Death Displacement

A time travel romantic thriller

Holly Copella

To my sister, Denise--
For enduring years of endless plots, characters, and storytelling

ACKNOWLEDGMENTS

Copella Books: First Paperback Edition June 2015
Cover Artist: Lori
SelfPubBookCovers.com/Lori
Printed by CreateSpace, An Amazon.com Company

PUBLISHER'S NOTE

Holly Copella

Chapter One

$\mathcal{T}$he forest was peaceful in the early morning. It was a crisp, clear morning leading into another sunny, warm day. The weather was perfect for the couple's early morning hike. A meek looking man in his early forties, Hayes Dante, walked along the worn path on the steep hillside with an attractive, dark-haired woman in her early twenties, Riley Jericho. Hayes, a well-respected curator for the local museum, looked almost out of place in the rugged wooded setting. Looks were deceiving though. Despite his city boy appearance, Hayes' reputation as an archaeologist and world explorer was well-established among his peers. Riley, his young assistant, had been at his side longer than anyone could remember. Despite having graduated college just one year earlier, she'd been a permanent fixture around the museum long before Hayes was hired as curator. Her youthful appearance led most to believe she was a naïve little girl, but behind those pretty brown eyes was a woman of great intelligence that none could deny.

Hayes appeared to be soaking in the atmosphere of the majestic, serene woodlands. A grin was chiseled onto his face. His resemblance of an evil mastermind was almost frightening. "This is nice; just the two of us."

Riley eyed him sharply from where she walked alongside him and appeared suspicious. Obviously, she knew the evil mastermind better than most. "Please tell me you didn't leave *her* behind just to get me out here alone."

He appeared humored by the comment and cast a sideways look at her. He was grinning a little too much. "To do what? Seduce my lovely, barely legal assistant?" he asked then chuckled while casually taking in his surroundings. "A lovely image, but I'm not that devious." He then appeared curious and again looked at her. "You are legal, aren't you?"

Riley hid her smile in an attempt to discourage his bad behavior, but she obviously didn't mind. "Your cracks about my age are becoming old," she scoffed then smiled teasingly, "you know, sort of like you."

He chuckled to the comment. "Oh, that's a new one."

Hayes' feelings for his young, attractive assistant were no secret. She knew; he knew; the entire museum knew. Rather than pretend his feelings didn't exist, they preferred the obvious jokes about it. There was speculation that he felt fatherly toward her, but that simply wasn't the case. He'd been in love with her since she was barely legal. She'd spent most of her life hanging out at the museum and charmed her way into his once cold existence. She changed his life in every possible aspect. Some might argue that she acquired her position as his assistant because he was so much in love with her, but no one could deny Riley's knowledge and love for the museum. It was her second home since she was a little girl. They walked several minutes in silence. Hayes continued to take in the scenery. Riley glanced at her older boss several times, and her mood seemed to change drastically. She suddenly became uncomfortable, but he hadn't even noticed.

"How much longer?" Riley asked, finally breaking the silence, and looked anywhere but at her boss.

Hayes removed the map from his pocket and examined it with great seriousness. "Well, according to the innkeeper's map, we're over halfway to the cave," he informed her. With the way he studied the map and the arching of his brows, he was undoubtedly calculating mathematical equations in his head. "We'll be there in under an hour."

Riley grabbed Hayes' arm and abruptly stopped him. He appeared surprised by her forcefulness as he looked up from his map and was about to question it when rocks slid out from beneath his feet. He looked down. The trail was completely washed away, leaving a deep, ten-foot wide crevice. The crevice was rocky and led down a frightening thirty-foot embankment. It would have definitely been a wrong step.

Hayes appeared horrified as he stared into the drop. "Is that what the innkeeper meant by a little washed out?"

Riley uncertainly looked around and appeared defeated by their lack of options. The hillside above them was equally steep as the hillside below them.

"I don't see any way around it," she informed him while groaning softly then studied his serious profile. "It's your call, Hayes."

Hayes assessed the surrounding area then the crevice itself. There were several larger, secure boulders just four feet below. "We'll need to take our time crossing," he informed her and returned the map to his pocket.

"Are you sure?" she asked and appeared tense. She gave him a firm look then attempted to hide her insecurities by teasing with him. "You're not nearly as spry as you used to be."

Hayes rolled his eyes with his disgust evident. "I was rock climbing before you were born," he scoffed. "You just try and keep up with me, little girl."

Her comment had obviously offended him. He usually reserved the 'little girl' name-calling for only special occasions. She didn't actually mean to offend him; she just didn't like the way the drop looked. It didn't seem safe. Hayes climbed down the four-foot drop to the rocky crevice then extended his hands to Riley. She smiled at her chivalrous boss.

"You're such the gentleman," Riley teased.

She placed her hands on his shoulders and allowed him to hold onto her waist while assisting her coordinated jump into the gully. She landed on the large rock with him. He kept his hands on her waist longer than he should and grinned slyly.

"I'd rather be tall," he replied.

Hayes held her hand as they carefully walked across the larger rocks to the other side. He obviously took it upon himself to look after his young assistant. Or perhaps he just enjoyed holding her hand. Smaller rocks tumbled down from the steep hillside above. Hayes must have felt the urgency and pulled her along more quickly. A thunderous rumble vibrated the ground and shot fear through them both. Riley looked up the hillside. Hayes suddenly grabbed her and forcibly shoved her up onto the ledge above them. She rolled from her hip onto her knees and reached for his extended hand. Their fingers touched. A landslide of rocks struck Hayes and took him down the embankment. Riley screamed and watched in horror as he tumbled among the rocks and vanished within the cloud of dirt. There was a moment of eerie silence. As the dust cleared, only rocks and dirt were visible below. Riley stared paralyzed only a moment before jumping from the ledge after him. She slid down the embankment, lost her footing, and tumbled several feet. A whirlwind of rocks was all Riley saw before striking the bottom. She lie motionless a moment from possible pain to every inch of her body. She slowly moved to her knees and could barely see through the blood running past her eye. She bled profusely from a deep gash above her blood-soaked eye and down her cheek. Despite the blood soaking her eye, she scanned the area.

"Hayes! Hayes!" Riley cried out.

There was no response. All sounds appeared to cease. Even the sounds from the forest were mysteriously silent. A dirty, bloodied hand was seen between some rocks. Riley hurriedly tossed rocks aside despite her own bleeding, cut hands. She removed a majority of the rocks surrounding Hayes' head and chest. Hayes didn't move and was soaked in dirt and blood. Beyond the thick layer of dirt, his severe chest injuries were frightening. He was seemingly crushed beneath the rocks. Riley gently attempted to wake him while fighting her tears.

"Hayes?"

He didn't respond. Riley removed her backpack and pulled out the hand radio. She pressed the talk button.

"Hello? Hello? I need help!"

There was no response or even sound from the radio. Riley stared at the radio and appeared stunned. Hayes suddenly gasped and coughed up blood.

Riley grasped his hand and moved closer to him. "Hayes, can you hear me?"

Hayes opened his eyes but appeared weak and pale. "Riley?" he wheezed and attempted to look at her. "Are you okay?"

She stared at him with the fear evident in her eyes then quickly sprang into action. "I'm going to get you out of here," she said firmly with renewed determination and began tossing aside more rocks. "Can you move?"

"The radio--"

She stopped moving rocks and looked at him as if the world had ended. Reality was setting in. "It's not working," she replied softly while fighting her tears.

"Go back to the inn," he weakly said.

She again took his hand, this time holding it between both of hers. "I won't leave you."

"I'll be fine," he gently told her. "It doesn't even hurt. Go get help."

Riley stared at Hayes' injuries and clung to his hand as blood tinged tears streaked her dirty, bleeding face. She knew he wouldn't be fine, and the fact that he wasn't in pain reinforced her worst fears. She sniffed and managed a tiny smile.

"I'm just going to stay with you another minute, okay?" she said softly while choking on her words.

Hayes weakly squeezed her hand and smiled tenderly as his eyes closed. "Okay--"

He wheezed softly as more blood seeped from his mouth. Hayes gasped for air. His hand relaxed as he exhaled softly. The legendary Hayes Dante was dead. Riley stared in horror then sobbed while clinging to him.

"No, Hayes, please don't do this to me."

Chapter Two

$\mathcal{F}$ive years later. The charming bedroom was tastefully decorated with exquisite antique furniture from the bed to the bedside table lamps. Light seeped into the bedroom through the partially open blinds. A ruggedly handsome man in his mid-thirties, Kane Maddox, clung to a woman while spooned against her beneath the covers. He woke, nuzzled the woman in his arms with a contented smile, and affectionately kissed the back of her neck. The attractive thirty-year-old woman, Selena Benton, turned with a weary smile and caressed his broad chest. Her lengthy blonde hair was pleasantly mussed and seemingly cascaded across her shoulders.

"Someone's up early," Selena cooed.

Kane chuckled softly while kissing her neck. "What do you intend to do about it?"

Selena smiled and kissed him passionately. Kane returned the kiss, rolled her onto her back, and firmly ran his hands along her thigh. It was going to be another beautiful day. Selena giggled then looked at the bedside clock and appeared alarmed.

"Is that the time?"

Kane kissed her shoulders while grinning deviously. "So you'll be a few minutes late," he teased.

Selena smirked and firmly tapped his shoulder. He groaned, lifted his head, and met her disapproving gaze.

"I'm not allowed to be late," she informed him. "It comes with being in charge."

Kane wasn't about to let that interfere with his morning plans. "I'm in charge, and I don't mind being late," he teased and returned to kissing her neck and throat.

She more firmly pushed against his shoulders. He groaned and rolled off her. She sat up, lovingly caressed his chest, and smiled sweetly.

"You'll just have to hold that thought until tonight," she informed him then sprang up from the bed before he could make another attempt to keep her there.

As he watched the sexy woman in the lacy, black nightgown head into the bathroom, he rolled onto his side and propped himself on his elbow. "I will!" he called after her.

Selena's giggle was heard in response as the bathroom door closed. Kane groaned and collapsed onto his back. He stared at the ceiling with a defeated look.

"Not even married yet, and I'm already reduced to taking cold showers."

✝

*M*addox Antiquities was a large, two-story antique store in the quiet, small town of Crestwood Village. The building itself was historic and dated back to the seventeen hundreds. Originally a gristmill, the building had been painstakingly restored by Kane's great grandparents when they first opened the antique store. The store had been passed down through the generations. Kane had bought the store from his parents in recent years to allow them the freedom to travel. The tastefully cluttered front room was filled with expensive antique furniture and various objects of similar value. Anything under a certain age or of lower value was typically sold at auctions, leaving only the finest antiques available. Customers traveled great distances to visit the store and check out the valuable pieces it contained. A stout man in his mid-thirties, Casper Finn, stood behind the desk while holding his cell phone to his ear.

"No kidding? That's awesome. Thanks, dude," Casper said with enthusiasm.

Casper disconnected the call and watched as Kane approached from the back room with a paper in his hand and a distracted look on his face. He didn't even bother looking at Casper as he approached the front desk.

"I know I'm fighting a losing battle on wedding flowers and centerpieces, but can napkins and matchbooks really cost this much?" Kane asked while staring at the invoice in disbelief. His wedding was costing him a fortune.

"Face it, man," Casper remarked while attempting to hide his devious grin. "Between Selena and your mother, you have no say in your own wedding. Do the smart thing. Just smile and write the checks. You'll thank me for it later."

Kane finally looked at Casper and appeared defeated. "Spoken like a true best man."

Casper appeared particularly playful to his best friend's turmoil. "If you're finished mourning the loss of your savings account, you have to check out the stuff I picked up this morning at the estate sale."

Kane casually looked over the objects scattered on top of the desk. Nothing caught his attention. Just more junk for the auction. Casper had an eye for junk, it seemed. Kane picked up an old journal and appeared disinterested.

"Old but not exactly treasure."

"It was a box deal," Casper announced then picked up one of the objects and looked over it with great interest. "This was what got my attention."

He proudly handed Kane the copper trinket box with strange carvings and changeable dates on it. Kane groaned lowly and barely looked at it.

"Not another trinket box."

Casper seemed surprised that Kane didn't share his enthusiasm. "It's inscribed with Latin."

"Just because something has Latin on it doesn't make it old or valuable," Kane informed him. "You know that."

"I'm telling you, it's some sort of ancient calendar," Casper announced as his excitement returned. "My Latin is a little rusty, so it may take some time to translate it."

Kane carelessly tossed him the trinket box. Casper gasped and caught it.

"You have fun with that," Kane remarked and sighed deeply, once again returning to the invoices he held. "I'll be in my office pricing limousines."

ϯ

*T*he iconic landmark museum situated in the middle of town encompassed the entire city block. It was set twenty feet from the street with towering pillars and an eye-catching sign displayed between them. Young schoolchildren held hands while following their teacher into the building in a long chain. Selena, dressed business casual, walked through the massive stone and marble lobby toward the large main desk with several workers surrounding it. The receptionist, Chrissie, was an attractive woman in her early thirties. She wore a stunning dress and daringly high, strapless heels. She was possibly the only employee who could get away with such uncomfortable shoes. Chrissie talked with one of the tour guides, Jillian, who wore the signature museum jacket, black pants, and conservative, comfortable shoes. Tour guides had the daunting task of covering miles of museum ground every day, and improper footwear could mean sudden death, especially on fieldtrip days. Jillian maintained a pleasant smile while she awaited the approaching children. The noise level was unusually loud because of all the children and their chaperones attempting to get them to settle down. No one envied the tour guides during school outings. One of the security guards, Tucker Hall, greeted Selena with his usual, pleasant smile.

"Good morning, Selena," he announced with a gentle tip of his hat.

Selena smiled but kept their greeting professional. "Good morning, Tucker."

"Collin was looking for you," he informed her. "Sounded important."

"Everything is important to Collin," she replied while sorting through a stack of mail lying on top of the desk.

Tucker continued to watch her while grinning, but she refused to look at him. Tucker was an undeniably handsome, muscularly built man in his early thirties. He seemed to pay a little too much attention to Selena, despite her obvious lack of interest. The museum curator in his late forties, Collin Morgan, approached with a file. Selena noted his fast gait and determined expression. Something had him concerned, but that was Collin's usual state.

"Morning, Collin," Selena said with a forced sound of cheerfulness.

"Bad news, Selena," he immediately began before even reaching her. "Your assistant called in this morning--"

"Again?"

"She called in to say she quit."

Selena allowed her head to fall into her hands and groaned. It was going to be a rocky start to her morning. Collin handed her the folder.

"This is the list you wanted her to pull from storage," he announced callously. "The exhibit needs to be ready in two days. As executive assistant, it falls on you."

Selena accepted the file with little enthusiasm. "I can't believe she quit. I have so much to do before the wedding. Working late nights is the last thing I need."

"You still have a few weeks until your wedding. This will only take two days," he remarked with little concern for her personal problems. "We'll try to find you a new assistant as soon as possible."

She groaned with a sound of defeat. "I remember being a lot more ambitious when I was a trainee," Selena scoffed.

"You were fortunate enough to work with Riley Jericho and Hayes Dante. Things were a lot different back then," he informed her. "Those two were irreplaceable."

"Yes, they were quite the team," Selena remarked without looking at Collin.

It was obviously disheartening to be reminded that she clearly wasn't Riley. It wasn't easy living in Riley's shadow, particularly since she'd been gone so long, but her legacy still overshadowed everything Selena did.

"It's so sad what happened to her," Selena muttered softly while shaking her head.

"Senseless tragedy," Collin remarked as he placed his hands in his pockets. He appeared chilled by the conversation. "It seems almost surreal that she died so soon after Hayes' accident. What were the odds, really?"

"She did take his death rather hard," Selena informed him then gave him an odd look. "Maybe her accident wasn't so much an accident as a cry for help."

"Suicide? No, absolutely not," he announced firmly. "Riley wasn't the type."

"She was mourning and possibly not thinking straight," she replied. "An error in judgment, perhaps." Selena looked at the folder in her hand and sighed deeply. "I should probably get on this list. I have a long day ahead of me."

Selena hurried across the lobby while skimming the file in her hand. She frowned and shook her head with disgust. A man in his late thirties, Noble Winston, approached her with a folder in his hand. She saw him approaching with his attention focused on her. It was too late to pretend she didn't see him and turn a different direction. As she looked at the folder, she couldn't even force herself to smile. She immediately groaned with disgust.

"Please don't tell me that's for me," Selena whined softly as Noble paused before her.

"Good morning to you too," Noble announced cheerfully and handed her the folder. "I need you to review these, approve them, and return them to me before lunch."

Selena groaned softly and accepted the folder. "You've got to be kidding."

"I tried to be nice and pass them off to Collin, but he wanted no part of it," Noble informed her.

"He should," she replied with a tone resembling disgust. "These fundraisers are usually his deal. How do I get stuck with all the paperwork?"

"You're his assistant," Noble remarked with a hint of mocking. "He wants you to assist with this."

"Yeah, funny," she snapped and added the folder to her own. "I'll do my best."

"Before lunch," Noble reminded and continued on his way across the lobby.

Selena's cell phone chirped from somewhere on her body. She fumbled within her blazer pocket for her cell phone. Both folders fell to the floor, allowing the papers to scatter. She groaned with frustration and grabbed her cell phone without looking at the caller ID.

"Selena Benton, Assistant Curator," Selena said with a failed attempt at cheerful. As she listened to the caller, her expression immediately dropped. "Who is this?"

Chapter Three

Kane walked across the antique store with a tiny, older woman and guided her to the front door. She appeared pleased with her new purchase; or maybe it was Kane's attentiveness. The way she smiled at the attractive man made it difficult to tell. The antique store had a reputation for outstanding customer service. The Maddox family was known for their even temperaments, business style, and amazing charm. Kane was no exception.

"We'll have that armoire delivered to your house by Friday," he informed her with a smile that matched hers.

The older woman smiled at him and patted his hand. "You always take such good care of me, Kane," she said. "I wish my grandchildren were like you."

"We both know you're not old enough to have grandchildren," he teased with a grin.

"You're such a sweet boy," she said with a giggle, gave his hand an affectionate squeeze, and left the store.

Some men came across as snake charmers with such lines, but Kane enjoyed working with customers. He had a particular fondness for little, gray-haired woman. Perhaps it was because they loved him so much. He had an amazing relationship with his grandmother on his mother's side up until her death a few years ago. She was a great influence on him growing up. Moreover, it didn't hurt that she was an exceptional baker. Casper hurried toward him with the old journal in his hand and excitement on his face.

"Dude, you're not going to believe this!" Casper said.

"Try me."

Casper was easily excited over the most mundane things. The two had been best friends ever since the day Casper kept a bully from beating Kane on the playground back in the third grade. His reason for coming to Kane's aid was the most ironic part. He liked the superhero on Kane's tee shirt, which was also the same reason the bully had wanted to beat him up in the first place. It was one of those things not worth trying to understand.

"I've dated the journal. It's over two hundred years old," Casper announced. "It didn't belong to the old man; it belonged to a different, much older man."

"Was he someone famous?" Kane asked dryly in an attempt to curb Casper's enthusiasm. "Because that still doesn't make that old journal worth anything."

"No, no. The journal explains the trinket box. You're not going to believe it. This is no ordinary trinket box I found," he said as his eyes glowed with excitement. "It's used for time displacement."

"Time displacement?" Kane was now convinced Casper was just making up words for his own amusement. "You'll need to explain that one to me."

"Time travel."

Kane stared at Casper with a strange but all too familiar look. "I think you've read one too many comic books," he informed him then sighed drearily. "If you don't mind, I have to see a man about white doves."

Kane walked across the store toward the front desk with Casper on his heels. He wasn't about to let it go.

"I'm not making this up!"

"Oh, well, in that case, go back in time and talk me into eloping."

"It doesn't work that way," Casper informed him. "It's a one-way ticket. The box remains in the present day, so there's no way to return."

"Hmm, well, that's screwed up. Who'd want to time travel and be stuck wherever they went?" Most times, Kane didn't mind humoring Casper's eccentric personality, but this was a little much. "Besides, that overpriced trinket box is not a time machine. It's barely even a trinket box."

"At least give it a try."

The look on Kane's face was priceless. "Give it a try?" he asked with surprise then laughed. "I wouldn't want to be anywhere other than here and now. I'm marrying the woman I love in a couple of weeks. My life is perfect." Kane rummaged through the desk and removed several proposals for wedding related items. "Well, it will be, if I survive the wedding planning."

"I'll do it," Casper chirped.

"Do what?" Kane asked without looking at his friend.

"Time travel," he replied.

Kane snorted a laugh at his odd friend. "You're my best man. Please don't make me replace you last minute," he said and barely paid attention to him. "I'm stressed enough as it is."

Casper stared at him and frowned his displeasure. "Now you're just mocking me."

Kane grinned his response. Casper's enthusiasm quickly returned. It was hard keeping Casper down.

"I'm going to prove this box makes time travel possible," Casper announced. "I'm going to travel forward in time by five minutes. You'll see."

"Okay, fine," Kane said with little emotion while preoccupied with the stack of proposals he flipped through.

Casper adjusted the date and time on the box, held it in his hand, and read from the book. Kane headed into the back room while shuffling through his papers. He returned only a minute later while holding up one of the papers and was about to speak. Casper was gone. He uncertainly looked around. The trinket box lie on the antique, Oriental rug on the floor.

"Casper?"

Kane walked behind the desk and looked for Casper. It was amazing how quickly and silently a man of Casper's size was able to move. As he turned, Casper stood in the middle of the room. Casper uncertainly picked up the trinket box from the floor then looked at Kane with enthusiasm.

"Well, did it work?" Casper asked.

Kane appeared bewildered. "Huh? Oh, yeah, sure. Uh, huh."

Casper frowned his displeasure.

Kane suddenly thought of something and groaned softly. "Damn, I need to call the photographer. You should see the price of these guys."

Kane left the room with his nose buried in his stack of papers. Casper looked at the trinket box and frowned. The clock struck three. He looked at his watch. It was five minutes before three. Casper's eyes widened with surprise.

"It worked," he gasped.

✝

*S*elena worked on one of the exhibits within the Egyptian room. It was already closing time and the museum was finally quiet. Selena appeared preoccupied by something while sorting through several items for the exhibit scattered along the floor. The sound of footfalls was heard, alerting her. Selena quickly spun and nearly collided with the night security guard, Howard. Both jumped with surprise. Howard laughed softly and held his chest. Howard was fairly out of shape despite only being in his mid-forties. If called upon to jump into action, he wouldn't be able to jump very far. Thankfully, his job wasn't very demanding. Selena's uneasiness wasn't typical behavior even while alone in the evening.

"You're a little edgy tonight," he announced while attempting to control his breathing and forced a smile.

Selena attempted to relax, laughed nervously, and ran trembling fingers through her long hair. "I could say the same about you, Howard."

"I'm not exactly used to things moving around in here," he replied while grinning. "I'm ready to lock up. Did you want me to walk you out to your car?"

"No, that's okay," she announced then sighed softly and finally appeared less tense. "I'm afraid I have another hour's worth of work tonight."

"Another late night?"

"My assistant quit," she replied while sulking.

"Another one?" he suddenly asked with surprise then shook his head. "What's with kids these days?" His jovial expression again returned. "Well, when you're ready to leave, call me, and I'll walk you out."

"I appreciate that, but Kane's coming to get me around eight," she informed him. "He worries when I work late."

Howard offered a knowing smile. "Nothing wrong with that in a future husband."

"No, nothing at all," she replied and returned the smile while subconsciously playing with her antique engagement ring.

"I'll leave you to your work," he announced cheerfully. "I wouldn't want to be the reason you have to stay even later then you already are."

Selena laughed softly, but it was obvious something still had her unhinged. Howard didn't seem to notice and continued on his way across the exhibit.

Chapter Four

*I*t was almost eight o'clock and the museum was closed for the evening. The lobby was dimly lit, lending a creepy appearance to the massive room. There was nothing creepier than the museum after hours. When it was quiet and the exhibits were mostly dark, shadows were cast, and one's imagination was projected back into time when dinosaurs roamed the earth. Kane stood outside the glass doors and rang the bell. Howard saw Kane at the main door from across the lobby, grinned as he approached, and opened the door for him. Howard had gotten to know Kane well since he started dating Selena and frequently came to pick her up when she worked late. All the employees knew one another and even frequently socialized outside of work with spouses and significant others. Kane entered and smiled at the guard.

"Evening, Kane," Howard greeted him cheerfully.

"Hey, Howard." Kane looked around the dim, quiet lobby and shook his head. Afterhours in the dimly lit museum always caused the hairs on the back of Kane's neck to stand on end. He didn't know how Howard could tolerate staying there alone every night. "Aren't you worried one of those dinosaurs will come back to life and eat you?"

"Be serious, Kane," Howard announced then grinned. "I'd have a heart attack long before one of those walking skeletons could ever eat me."

Kane chuckled. The image was one he was sure Casper would enjoy. "Is Selena ready?"

"I don't know, but you need to take that girl home. She works too hard for someone so young."

"I hear you. Unfortunately, she makes more here than what I could pay her at the antique store," Kane replied with a defeated sigh. "Where is she?"

"In the Egyptian exhibit, I believe."

"Thanks, Howard."

Kane walked through the dinosaur exhibit and looked around with a grimace. The shadows reflected by the large dinosaur skeletons were enough to quicken his pace. He hated to admit that the place gave him chills. It seemed childish. He headed into the Egyptian exhibit. The massive, dimly lit room was filled with mummies in glass cases, sarcophaguses, and various scenes from Egypt. Kane entered the eerie room. The mummies were possibly less comforting than the dinosaur skeletons. As he stared at a mummy beyond a glass case, he didn't envy Howard at all. A gunshot was heard and echoed throughout the room. Kane was paralyzed a moment while considering if he had actually heard a gunshot. Alarm swept through him. Kane ran across the exhibit and suddenly stopped. Selena was lying on the floor with blood soaking her shirt and a gun near her outstretched hand. Kane ran for her and dropped alongside her. He grabbed her hand and pat if firmly. A flood of emotion swept over him as he stared at the woman he loved bleeding before him.

"Selena, Selena! Talk to me!"

Selena gasped as if about to speak but no words came out. Her eyes rolled back, and she stopped breathing. Kane gasped with horror while staring at her. He suddenly sobbed and pulled her into his arms.

"No, Selena!"

Out of the corner of his eye, he saw someone move through the shadows. Kane suddenly grabbed the gun, jumped to his feet, and prepared to shoot the first thing that moved. To his surprise, the gun was kicked from his hand with amazing force. He stared Selena's killer in the eyes. It was Riley Jericho! Kane stared at the woman he'd never seen before and appeared unable to move. She had a noticeable scar above her right white, blind eye and down her cheek. She was dressed in a black slinking outfit and her dark hair was pulled back into a ponytail. Kane lunged for the woman with rage. She kicked him in the chest with her black booted foot and knocked him backwards. She casually turned to leave. Kane clutched his chest with agony and stared after her. He wasn't about to let Selena's killer get away. Without thinking, he again lunged for her while her back was turned. Scarred Riley spun into a backwards roundhouse kick and hit him across the face. Kane roughly struck the floor and appeared unable to move. Scarred Riley slowly approached Kane and crouched alongside him as he writhed in agony and clutched his bleeding cheek. He gasped and looked at her. The scar on her face and her white, blind eye were intimidating, and he allowed the fear that she'd kill him overtake him. Despite his pain, he was paralyzed with fear and stared helplessly at her. She casually stared into his eyes and showed no emotion.

"I'm sorry for your loss, Kane," she remarked simply.

Kane stared at her emotionless expression as a shiver ran down his spine. He was sure he was dead. Howard was heard running into the exhibit. Kane had to alert Howard, even if it meant the woman would kill him. He slowly and painfully looked across the room as Howard entered the exhibit. He had his hand on his gun, although if he'd heard the gunshot it should have already been in his hand.

"Howard!" Kane weakly cried out a warning from where he lie on the floor in agony.

Howard ran toward him while removing his gun from its holster. Kane looked back to Scarred Riley, wondering if it would hurt when she killed him. To his surprise, she was gone.

Chapter Five

It was two days later, and the following day was Selena's funeral. Kane sat in his office slumped over his desk with his head in his hands. He stared blankly at the framed engagement photo of him and Selena now streaked with dried tears. Images of the woman with the blind eye were permanently burned into his mind. He saw her face every time he shut his eyes. The cut she'd left on his cheek when she kicked him was a cruel reminder of his failed attempt to catch Selena's killer. He hated himself for having allowed the woman to take him down so easily. He couldn't admit to himself that he had been outmatched. Kane ran over the entire scene a thousand times and tried to think of something he could have done differently to stop the woman. He let her get away, and, for that, he couldn't forgive himself. His self-pity was interrupted by Casper's familiar, yet less jovial voice from the office doorway.

"Kane--" Casper said softly from within the open doorway, nearly choking on his own emotions.

Kane didn't even bother looking up. He just clung to his head and stared at the photo. "If it's my parents, I don't feel like talking," he barely muttered.

"It's Detective Perkins."

Kane suddenly looked up with anticipation as his heart raced. Casper stood alongside a middle-aged man in an inexpensive suite. Detective Perkins was the stereotypical image of a police detective straight from any number of police shows. He was almost certainly more capable than he looked. At least, Kane hoped that was the case. Casper lowered his head and left him alone with the detective. Kane slowly stood as Perkins entered.

"Did you find her?" he gasped almost too quickly while clutching the edge of the desk with anticipation.

"No, I'm sorry," Perkins announced gently.

Kane felt his entire body sink. He felt as if his legs would give out. He collapsed into his chair.

"I'd like you to have a look at a photo," Perkins continued with some reluctance.

Perkins placed a photo on the desk. Kane looked at the picture before him. It was a picture of Riley taken after the accident, which revealed her scar and blind eye. Kane grabbed the photo with the alarm evident on his face and bolted up from his chair.

"That's her! That's the woman who killed Selena!" It was the first time his heart rate had risen since that night. He'd been deep in a fog since Selena's murder. He could feel his body twitch with redemption for her death.

"I was afraid of that," Perkins said gently and lacked the enthusiasm Kane was hoping he'd show. "Her name *was* Riley Jericho."

"Was?" Kane felt his heart sink. He knew it was her, and she certainly wasn't a ghost.

"There was a boating accident five years ago," he announced. "Her body was never found."

"That's her! That scar and her white eye are burned into my mind forever," Kane firmly announced while shaking the photo. He felt himself ready to explode. "She's not dead!"

"And I believe you," he announced while frowning. "We didn't find anything at the museum. The security cameras were tampered with, so we have little to go on. It was too neat."

"Why would she kill Selena?" he suddenly blurted out. "Was it a robbery gone bad?"

"More like a friendship gone sour," Perkins informed him. "Riley used to work with Selena before the accidental death of their boss, Hayes Dante. She was his assistant, which explains how she was able to get around the museum undetected. She knew every inch of that place."

Kane stared at the detective and felt oddly confused by what he was hearing. Something didn't add up. "Selena never mentioned either of them."

"I suppose that's not surprising. Riley went off the deep end after Dante's death," Perkins said. "It was only a month or so later that she had her accident; or should I say apparently staged her accident."

"So she's insane?"

The detective scratched his head and shrugged. "That's the best we have to go on, I'm afraid."

"So you have no idea where she could be?"

"We're checking security cameras around the museum, but so far we haven't come up with anything useful," Perkins informed him. "She was very careful."

His words and tone offered little comfort to Kane. "Even if they had a falling out, why would she want to kill Selena?" Kane suddenly asked. "You just said it's been five years since anyone's seen her."

"We have so little information to go on, but the current curator, Collin, said that Riley's anger with Selena began after Dante's death," the detective informed him. "It's possible she, for some reason, blamed Selena for the accident."

"Selena never mentioned them or any of this," Kane said. "How did Hayes Dante die?"

"Rockslide during an expedition to an archaeological find in the backwoods about two hours from here," Perkins informed him. "Obviously there's no possible way your girlfriend was involved. It was an accident of nature, plain and simple."

Kane once again felt his heart ache. "You're not convinced you'll find her, are you?"

Perkins sighed and appeared defeated. "This woman staged her own death five years ago and remained a ghost all these years. Our only evidence that she's alive and killed your girlfriend is your testimony. Tracking her down isn't going to be easy. We have nothing to go on and no place to start."

"What about the gun she used?"

"Untraceable. The only fingerprints on the gun were Selena's and yours. There must have been a struggle for control of the gun." Detective Perkins stared at Kane a long moment before giving a sigh of defeat. "Riley Jericho knew what she was doing. We're dealing with a highly intelligent, extremely unpredictable and unstable woman."

"You forgot to mention dangerous," Kane informed him and gingerly touched the injury on his cheek. "She had me on the ground before I even knew what hit me."

"The fact that she didn't kill you is both puzzling and reassuring," Perkins replied. "I believe she took out what she considered to be her intended target. You were very lucky. If she wanted you dead, you would be."

"Who says I'm not dead?"

Chapter Six

It was later that same afternoon. Kane busily worked on the computer at his desk. He appeared completely engrossed in his research and didn't even notice Casper had entered. Casper stood behind Kane and stared at the computer screen over his shoulder. There were articles about Hayes Dante's accidental death scattered along the desk and an article on Riley's boating accident on the computer. The same photo the detective had shown him appeared on the screen.

"What are you doing?" Casper asked.

Kane jumped with surprise and looked back at his friend. He didn't know how a man of his size could move so quietly. He considered tying a bell around his neck.

Casper stared at the image of Riley on the computer screen and appeared alarmed while gasping, "Isn't that the woman who killed Selena?"

Kane returned to the screen with a hardened look on his face. "Detective Perkins is holding out little hope of finding her, so I'm going to find her myself."

The look on Casper's face expressed his horror to the idea. "The next time you run into her, you may not survive the experience," Casper firmly announced then appeared more sympathetic and placed his hand on Kane's shoulder. "Why don't you go home? It's getting late and, you know, the funeral's tomorrow--"

Kane groaned softly and sank in his chair while holding his head. "I keep going over it in my head," he said softly. "If I had only gotten there sooner. One minute would have done it. Just one, lousy minute."

"You can't change the past, dude."

He suddenly sat up straight and looked at Casper with all seriousness. "What if I could?"

It took Casper a minute to catch on. "You mean the old man's time machine?" he asked with surprise then shook his head. "One-way trip, remember. Besides, she nearly killed you. What makes you think you can stop her?"

"No one says I have to stop her," he announced. "I'm not talking about going back two days. What if I went back five years and took Selena away before her boss dies? Remove her from the equation." Kane felt invigorated for the first time since Selena's murder. "She can't blame Selena for Dante's accident if she wasn't even there."

"Time travel is tricky business. You can't risk running into your past self."

"I only met Selena two years ago, so there's not risk of running into my past self in her circle," he reminded his friend. "Can it work?"

"I don't know. The museum is just a few blocks from here." Casper then appeared to consider what Kane was contemplating and gave it serious thought. "If you really want to do this, you're going to need my help, but first you'll need to convince me you're not crazy."

Kane gave him an odd look. "How's that?"

"Not me," Casper announced and gestured with his hands. "The *other* me."

Kane nodded with understanding. "Oh, you mean *you* from the past."

"Yeah," Casper informed him. "I've mellowed considerably over the last five years. I've changed a lot. I'm more open-minded these days. Me from the past may not believe that whole time travel stuff."

"You've changed?" Kane suddenly asked and attempted to hide his smile although a soft snicker escaped. "Please, you haven't changed since the third grade."

"That's offensive, dude."

A tiny smile crossed his face. "Remember the time I convinced you my bedroom closet was haunted?" Kane teased.

"Yeah, I was twelve," Casper scoffed.

Kane cleverly raised his brow and felt particularly playful. "What about the time I told you about the aliens living in the toolshed? You hid under a tarp for three nights in a row attempting to get a picture of them."

"You were such a rotten, little boy," Casper scoffed while shaking his head. He then appeared to reconsider. "But you did get me a date with Chelsea in Dr. Melbourne's class. I guess that sort of made up for the rest."

"You still owe me for that," Kane muttered.

There was a moment of silence while Casper appeared deep in thought. "I'll need some time to map out our plan of attack to keep you from running into your past self while looking for me."

"Anything I can do?"

"Bring those articles with you," he replied. "Me from the past may need them."

†

It was nearly midnight the following night and Selena's funeral had taken a lot out of Kane. Casper and Kane stood in the cluttered, dimly lit alley behind the museum. It was even creepier than the exhibits within the museum. There was very little activity that late at night in their small town, which actually worked to their advantage. Casper fiddled with the copper trinket box while Kane looked around with bewilderment.

"Why did you choose here of all places?" Kane asked and immediately felt chilled. He didn't want to be reminded of what happened there.

"Logistics. No one will be here this time of night, my apartment is just down the street, and you're far enough away from the store that you won't run into your past self," Casper informed him. He handed Kane a photo. "Here's a picture to prove to me you're from the future."

Kane placed the photo in his jacket pocket without looking at it. He was already tense and having second thoughts. If it didn't work, he'd feel even worse.

"Is this really going to work?"

"I guess that depends on how convincing you are with Selena," Casper replied with a shrug of his shoulders. "There's really no telling with women. If I understood them, I'd probably have a steady girlfriend."

"No, I mean *this*, time travel," Kane stated firmly. "I'm feeling a little stupid."

"You want to be with Selena, don't you? You have to trust me," Casper informed him then gave him a stern, serious look. "There's a flash of light, so I recommend you close your eyes." Casper handed him the trinket box set to five years ago. "This will place you exactly one week before the accident that kills Hayes Dante. That should give you enough time to work your magic with Selena from the past. When you're ready, just push the two buttons simultaneously."

Casper took a step back and gave him two thumbs up. Kane studied the trinket box a moment, inhaled deeply, pressed both buttons, and shut his eyes. He felt a strange pulling on his body, and his joints suddenly ached. Kane slowly opened his eyes and saw Casper still standing in front of him wearing the same shirt. He had a strange look on his face. Kane groaned with disgust and shook his head.

"It didn't work--"

He didn't know why he trusted Casper. It was the Ouija board incident all over again.

"What didn't work?" Casper asked. "What are you doing in an alley?"

Kane rolled his eyes. His friend had a warped sense of humor. Given the circumstances of the last few days, he'd think Casper would have a little more sympathy for the situation and not insist on tormenting him now. He was seriously considering finding a new best friend.

"Very funny, Casper," Kane scoffed. "I'm really not in the mood."

Casper stared at him as if not understanding his response. "Dude, are you drunk?" he asked with a look of concern on his face. "We'd better get you home."

Kane stared at Casper a moment and considered a rude outburst when he noticed the shirt his friend wore. It was the same shirt, but it appeared brand new. Kane uncertainly looked around for the trinket box. It was gone!

"Oh, my God! It did work!" Kane cried out.

Casper groaned softly, shook his head, and gently took Kane's arm. "We can't let your mother see you like this," he announced sternly. "I'll take you back to my place and let you sleep it off on my sofa."

Kane laughed as Casper led him from the alley. "I'll be damned, it worked. You're a genius, Casper!"

Casper shook his head with defeat. "I tried to warn you. This is what happens when you eat the worm."

Chapter Seven

Casper's studio apartment was small and cluttered, lending to the typical bachelor stereotype. Clean and dirty clothes were thrown haphazard together around the room. Even the kitchen wasn't immune to scattered clothing. Dirty dishes were piled high in the sink and it was quite possible there were more hiding in the oven. The apartment was furnished with antique irregulars. It was Casper's own term for antique furniture that was sadly beyond repair and would never again qualify as antique because of extensive, modern repairs. Kane attempted to make himself comfortable on the three-legged chaise, which had a stack of books piled beneath the corner where the fourth leg should be. Oddly enough, his friend still had the same sofa in the present day. It was still missing its leg five years from now. Actually, the entire apartment seemed exactly the same almost down to the empty take-out cartons. Kane found that to be a little disturbing. Casper sat on the severely sagging, red velvet sofa and stared at Kane with disbelief.

"Dude, what are you on?" Casper asked.

"It's true, Casper," Kane attempted to convince him. He couldn't believe how difficult a task it was convincing Casper of something he usually believed in. "If you went to my house, you'd find me there. Me--the other me."

"You mean your parents' house, dude."

"In a few years, I buy the shop and their house so they can retire and travel."

"Now I know you're on something," he scoffed. "You hate working in the store, and there's no way you're becoming my boss. I'd be miserable working for a prick like you."

Kane rolled his eyes and groaned softly. This wasn't going as well as he had anticipated. Casper lived for this sort of bullshit, and yet he wasn't even willing to believe it.

"Besides, with what your parents pay you, how could you possibly afford to buy the shop and their house?" Casper asked callously. "Did you win the lottery or something?"

"After Nana died--"

Casper suddenly appeared horrified and bolted upright. "Nana dies? Dude, I live for her pies!"

"She left me a sizeable inheritance," Kane continued. "I used that to buy the shop from my parents."

The look on Casper's face was unpredictable. "You should be ashamed of yourself," he suddenly grumbled while shaking his head. "Using your poor grandmother dying to make me believe another bullshit story meant to trick me. Remember the alien in your toolshed?"

Kane groaned softly and allowed his face to fall into his hands. The chaise wobbled severely beneath him.

"If one of you wasn't bad enough--" Kane muttered.

Something then occurred to Kane. He sat up straight, checked his jacket pocket, and removed the photo. He still had it! He handed the photo to Casper.

"You told me to give you this."

Casper accepted the picture and looked at it. It was of Kane, Selena, and Casper at a baseball game taken just a few months ago--although technically five years from now.

"Look at the date on the advertisement behind us," Kane announced. "It's five years from now."

Casper's eyes suddenly widened. "Dude, it's true!" he announced excitedly and his enthusiasm quickly escalated. "This is beyond awesome." He studied the picture a moment longer and grinned. "Who's the hot girl? Tell me she's mine."

Kane frowned and took the picture from him. He stared at Selena in the photo and held back his tears. "No, she was mine," he said softly. "She's the reason I'm here." He again looked at Casper with the hurt evident in his eyes. "I need to keep her from dying, and you're the only one who can help me."

"Yeah, sure. Anything to help," Casper announced without hesitation then appeared to consider and fidgeted. "Do you think it's too late to call Nana?"

Kane considered the question and snorted a soft laugh. "It's almost one o'clock in the morning," he remarked bluntly then smirked knowingly. "I'm sure she's still up cleaning closets or watching some gory horror movie."

As Casper reached for the phone, Kane smiled. It would be nice to hear her voice again. Would it be wrong to stop in for a slice of pie?

✝

*I*t was almost nine o'clock the next morning. The museum had swarms of children on the steps awaiting the official opening. They were excited to be anywhere other than in school. Teachers and chaperones attempted in vain to keep the children rounded up and together. The smaller the mastermind, the easier they would escape. Kane paced the sidewalk while Casper attempted to instruct him. In comparison, Casper's job today wasn't much unlike that of the teachers with their young, excitable children.

"You need to relax, dude," Casper announced. "She hasn't even met you yet." He shook his head. "I knew giving you coffee this morning was a bad idea."

"I can't relax. This is more stressful than our first date. There's so much riding on this meeting," he announced while nervously running his fingers through his dark hair. At this rate, he'd be bald before the museum even opened.

"Maybe, but you have home field advantage," Casper insisted and gave his shoulder a firm squeeze. "You already know everything about her. You'll win her over at 'hello'."

"I only have one week to convince her to go away with me before Dante's accident," Kane announced. "That's a lot of pressure, considering we dated almost three months before I convinced her to sleep with me."

"Really?" Casper asked with some surprise and stared longer than he should have. "Wow, that's just sad."

Kane glared at him. Casper caught his glare and appeared humored.

"Chill, I'm just messing with you. I need more time to work on your problem," he announced. "While you cozy up to your girl, I'll run a few scenarios in my head. Maybe you don't need to whisk her away for an entire week. Maybe you just need to take her away for one day." Casper's enthusiasm took over as if on cue. "I'll read those articles you brought from the future. There might be something in there we can use. You just find your girl and work your charm on her."

The museum doors finally opened and the children spilled inside like a massive flood of locust. Kane was even more tense now and alternated pacing and running fingers through his hair. His pounding heart wasn't helping.

"Relax. You'll be fine." Casper caught him by the shoulders and turned him in the direction of the museum door. He then grinned and gave him two thumbs up. "Good luck, dude."

Kane nervously nodded, took a deep breath, and hurried for the museum entrance behind the children. Casper watched him and shook his head. A frown crossed his face.

"He really needs a chaperone," he muttered. His cell phone rang. Casper hit a button and placed the cell phone to his ear. "You reached my voicemail. Please leave a message after the beep." Casper hesitated then made a beeping sound.

"Hey, Casper," came Kane's voice. "Where are you?"

Casper suddenly tensed then smiled and laughed. "Kane! What's up, dude?"

"You were supposed to be here half an hour ago," Kane said with a tone of irritation from the other end. "My father is on my case already."

"Uh, yeah, I'm in the car now," Casper said then grimaced as he hurried for his cherished, black Mustang parked at the curb a few feet away. "I'll be there in two minutes. I, uh, was just running an errand for, uh, *you*."

Kane entered the lobby behind the horde of schoolchildren and their chaperones. The noise within the lobby was almost deafening as children's chatter and the occasional shrill scream echoed off the high ceilings. Chrissie collected the admission fees for more than one hundred children from their accompanying chaperones. Kane patiently waited his turn to purchase an admission ticket. It seemed odd. This was the first time he'd ever actually had to pay for admission to the museum. He searched the lobby for Selena while he waited. With all the children and adults supervising them, it was difficult to make out any one face. As Kane reached the front desk, most of the children had cleared out into the first exhibit behind one of the tour guides. He paid his fee to Chrissie and stared at her a moment. Seeing her here and now seemed odd. He was almost surprised by how much younger she looked just five years ago. Kane resisted the urge to greet her by name and instead gave a generic smile and nod. Shortly after he passed, Jillian approached the desk, leaned on it, and vented to Chrissie.

Kane walked across the lobby and paused near a rack of brochures. He knew Chrissie and Jillian were notorious gossips. It seemed feasible to assume they may know where Selena was at that moment, so he decided to hang around and listen. He and Selena spent many Friday nights with those two at the local bar and the city comedy club. Chrissie was actually Selena's maid-of-honor. They'd gotten into a small tiff about bridesmaids' dresses a few months ago. If Chrissie had her way, the bridesmaids would all look like streetwalkers. Sometimes Selena was too much of a good girl and it got on Chrissie's nerves. Selena also wasn't very happy with him for gawking at the dresses with a grin chiseled on his face. He was usually a gentleman, but there were times it felt good being a bad boy. Deep down, he was sure Selena understood the 'boys will be boys' mentality. Considering how much she liked Casper, she had to understand.

"I can't believe we're going to be stuck here while the so called important people are running off to some romantic bed and breakfast for another field trip," Chrissie remarked.

"Yeah, seriously? How many of them does it take to check out an unconfirmed find?" Jillian announced with the disgust evident in her tone.

"It's just not fair," Chrissie whined. "I should have had that promotion years ago. Instead I'm stuck at the desk and running errands for Collin."

Kane suddenly became interested. If he could locate Collin, he'd almost certainly find Selena. He looked at the brochure in his hand and frowned. He probably stared at that brochure long enough. It seemed as if the museum was having a fundraiser on Friday night. He swore they were always having a fundraiser. Selena complained about them often. It always meant more work for her. Noble Winston was in charge of their fundraisers. Apparently, he wasn't exactly efficient in his job. Selena was always complaining that she often needed to fix his mistakes. Randy, a man in a maintenance uniform, approached the desk. Kane had never seen him before. He must have quit before Kane started dating Selena and got to know the museum employees. Randy stopped before the two women and appeared particularly impatient.

"Have either of you seen Selena?" he asked. "This work requisition makes no sense."

Kane listened more closely at the mention of Selena's name. Chrissie took the work request from him and looked at it. She groaned and rolled her eyes.

"Selena needs to work on her penmanship," Chrissie informed him. "She needs scaffolding in the Egyptian exhibit."

Randy took the paper from her, made a face, and studied it. "How do you get that from this?" he asked.

Both women laughed softly. Kane wasn't getting anywhere standing around the lobby. The Egyptian exhibit seemed a better place to start. He returned his brochures and headed for the next exhibit over.

Chapter Eight

*O*t was almost an hour later. Kane returned to the dinosaur exhibit, looked around with little interest, and glanced at his watch several times. He'd been in the museum over an hour and there was still no sign of Selena. He couldn't believe how anxious he was about running into her. They technically wouldn't even meet for another three years. He was having some concerns about forcing an accidental meeting. It seemed risky, but the way he saw it, there really was little alternative. When they first met, Selena was instantly taken with him. She was a bright moment in a dark time for him. It was only a few months after his grandmother had died that they'd first started dating. Selena made falling in love with her an effortless task. He knew she was the woman he'd marry after only a few short weeks of dating. Selena claimed she knew it by the end of their first date. He didn't believe in love at first sight. Maybe that was just because it had never happened to him. Whatever it was Selena felt after their first date, it proved women held some divine inspiration regarding relationships. He envied women for that. Small children ran around and caused a commotion while tour guides and teachers attempted to rein them in. Kane snapped out of his daze and watched the children buzzing past him. God, he wanted children of his own. The dream seemed so far away now. He suddenly collided with someone.

"I'm so sorry--" Kane began and then looked at the man standing before him.

Hayes Dante shook spilled coffee from his hand and managed a soft chuckle despite the hot sting. "I prefer to drink my coffee to wake up," he teased.

Kane stared at Hayes longer than he should have. It was almost eerie looking at a man about whose death he had just read. He was suddenly chilled. His smiling picture from the lengthy obituary was burned into Kane's mind. Kane shook the image of Hayes' obituary photo and fumbled slightly.

"Let me buy you another coffee," he announced while continuing to stare.

"No, it's okay, really." Hayes apparently realized Kane was staring at him and seemed bothered by the attention. "Is something wrong?"

"Uh, no," Kane said while fidgeting then quickly covered as best he could and managed a smile. "Aren't you Hayes Dante, the museum curator?"

"Yes, have we met before?"

Not if he didn't count his obituary photo. Kane again shook the image from his head and maintained his tense smile. "No, but I believe I saw you at a benefit a while back," Kane announced with more conviction. Selena slipped into his thoughts, allowing him to smile more naturally. "You were, uh, with a very attractive young woman, if I'm not mistaken."

Hayes' smile brightened considerably. "Oh, you noticed her, did you?" he asked with a soft chuckle and seemed pleased. "That would be my lovely assistant. Keeping her close is the only way I get noticed at those benefits."

"She's certainly distracting," Kane remarked. Selena had that effect on most men. He felt himself drifting back to thoughts of the woman he loved. In particular, he reminisced about the morning on the day she died. Kane wished he'd put more of an effort into keeping her in bed and desperately wished they'd made love that morning. He shook himself back into reality and smiled at Hayes. "Again, I'm really sorry about the coffee."

"I think I'll live."

Tucker, the security guard, approached Hayes while appearing all official. Kane marveled at how much younger Tucker looked than he remembered. He was a little beefier five years in the past. Apparently, Tucker worked out more when he was younger. Kane wished he took time to work out himself. Not that he was a slouch; he just wasn't muscular like Tucker was.

"Sorry to bother you, Hayes," Tucker announced with a tone of annoyance in his voice. "One of the little rug rats refunded on Homo erectus."

Hayes groaned and rolled his eyes. "It's going to be one of those mornings," he grumbled. "Find Selena. She'll be thrilled to hear the good news."

Kane tensed to hearing mention of Selena's name. His heart immediately pounded with anticipation. As Tucker walked away, Kane knew he had to follow him if he intended accidentally to run into her.

Hayes grinned while glancing back at Kane. "As you can see, having coffee spilled on me is quite a pleasant change of pace around here," he teased. "Enjoy your visit."

Hayes walked past Kane and continued on his journey. Kane quickly turned and followed Tucker from a safe distance. Tucker entered the lobby and approached the much younger, twenty-five-year-old Selena near the front desk. Kane stopped to stare at her as his heart pounded with excitement and tears welled in his eyes. Seeing her alive was all that suddenly mattered. He couldn't believe how good she looked, even if she did look younger than he remembered. As he stared at her, his entire body seemed to react to the sight of the woman he loved. He just wanted to pull her into his arms and never let her go. Thoughts of their last sexual encounter filled his head. He quickly pushed those thoughts aside. Tucker spoke to her from behind. Selena turned to face Tucker, smiled, and jumped into his arms. They kissed passionately. Kane suddenly froze as alarm swept through his entire body. It was something he hadn't taken into consideration when he traveled back in time to save Selena from being murdered in the future. She already had a boyfriend! Kane could barely watch Selena kissing another man without his body twitching with jealousy and possibly anger. When had she dated Tucker? She pulled away and smiled lustfully at the handsome, muscular man. Kane turned and hurried from the lobby. He walked briskly through the dinosaur exhibit and didn't slow until he entered the mummy exhibit. He finally stopped and collapsed on a secluded bench. He fought his tears while holding his head. His emotions were on a roller coaster, and he wasn't sure how much more he could physically take.

"Are you okay?" a woman's voice was heard from over him.

It was a familiar voice he knew he'd heard before. Kane wiped his eyes, composed himself, and looked up. The younger, non-scarred version of Riley stood over him. Shock and horror swept over him as he stared at the woman who five years from now murders his girlfriend. She was something he hadn't considered. He never considered the possibility of running into her. Then it dawned on him. Riley was the assistant Hayes spoke of so fondly! How could he forget something that important? His body twitched as every emotion he'd ever had exploded inside him. Rage from the night she murdered Selena began to surface.

"I, uh, yeah."

"This is usually when I ask if you need help finding your teacher," she teased with a grin, "but you seem a bit older than the usual lost child."

Kane stared at her and couldn't look away, although it wasn't her beauty that commanded his attention. All he saw was the monster who murdered Selena. He knew his expression was revealing too much. All the hurt and anger rushed to the surface in an uncontrollable tidal wave of emotion. He had to escape before he reacted in the worst possible way. He had to get away from her before his hands found their way to her throat.

"I, uh, excuse me."

Kane hurried for the nearest men's room and quickly entered. His heart raced and his entire body twitched as he paced the length of the restroom like a caged animal. He suddenly turned with rage and punched the mirror. It shattered across the sink and floor. Kane shook his hand with surprise and discomfort. Surprisingly, he hadn't cut himself. He wanted to scream out every expletive with fury, but he held them back. Kane didn't know how he was going to make this work. He couldn't charm Selena away from her boyfriend, Tucker of all people, while knowing Riley was in the same building. He wanted to kill Riley! Suppressing those feelings wasn't going to be easy. He considered his options as he stared at his reflection in the broken mirror. Oddly enough, he didn't recognize his own reflection.

✝

*K*ane quietly slinked through the Egyptian exhibit half an hour later and kept close watch for Riley. Several children screamed at one another while running amuck. He paused near one of the exhibits and looked across the room. There she was! Riley stood on the newly erected scaffolding and worked on one of the taller exhibits. He watched her and felt his blood boiling. He was standing in the same room where she later killed Selena. He looked at the exact spot on the floor and could almost see Selena dying in his arms. He looked back at Riley as she climbed the scaffolding to its highest point near the tall ceiling. For a brief moment, he considered the pleasure he would receive from knocking her off the scaffold and watching her to plummet to her death on the cold, marble floor. As more children ran past the conned off area, one of the heavier exhibits toppled from its base and struck the bottom scaffold leg. The scaffold rocked harshly, creaked, and broke apart. Kane jumped with surprise and alarm as the scaffold toppled with Riley on top. As the scaffold crashed to the floor with a thunderous clatter, Riley somersaulted through the air, seemingly haphazard. She landed almost gracefully in a half-crouched position like a panther falling from a tree. Kane stared at Riley's amazing, flying dismount while completely awestruck. The scaffold crashed across the marble floor. Riley uncertainly straightened as a crowd quickly gathered around her. Randy stopped before the pile of scaffolding and stared at it with shock. Hayes suddenly appeared and saw Riley near the disaster while brushing dirt from her pants. He ran to her and immediately checked her for injuries.

"Are you okay?" he asked with concern while barely giving her time to respond. "Where are you hurt?"

"I'm fine," Riley announced and appeared oddly unshaken by the entire incident.

"I don't know what--" Randy began.

Hayes immediately spun toward Randy with a look in his eyes that was indescribable. "What did you do?"

"I didn't do anything," Randy protested. "Everything was in perfect working order when I left it."

"Perfect working order?" Hayes proclaimed and pointed at the mess of metal and wood piled on the floor. "Does that look like it's in perfect working order to you? There are children running everywhere. One of them could have been under that when it collapsed. It nearly killed Riley!"

"But it didn't," Riley informed Hayes in a failed attempt to calm him.

"That's not the point!"

Everyone was now staring at Hayes with surprise. Riley looked sheepishly away then gently nudged Hayes, breaking his death stare on Randy. Hayes twitched slightly and appeared to calm on command to her touch.

Hayes collected himself, took a deep breath, and stared sternly at the maintenance man before him. "I believe you're finished here," he said calm but firm.

Randy stared at him with astonishment. "What? You can't do that!"

"I believe I just did," Hayes replied without emotion then turned and walked away.

Riley appeared almost as surprised as Randy was. As he fumed, she offered a sympathetic look then hurried after Hayes. Kane continued to watch the entire scene unfold from his position across the room. He couldn't believe how protective Hayes was over Riley. For a seemingly docile man, he had a frightening temper hidden within.

Chapter Nine

*T*here was limited activity and few people outside the museum after it closed for the evening. Casper's black Mustang was parked just down the street within viewing distance of the museum entrance. Casper sat behind the wheel while Kane stared out the window at the museum. Casper didn't appear convinced about their reason for being there that time of evening. He strummed the steering wheel with his chubby fingers, scanned the area beyond the windshield, and then finally looked at Kane, who sat ridged in the passenger seat.

"We're not stalking your girlfriend, are we? Because that's not cool," Casper finally announced in all seriousness.

Kane's eyes remained locked on the front doors of the museum. "No, I'm still working on a solution to the boyfriend problem, but something else came up that needs to be immediately dealt with," he said firmly.

"What's that?"

Kane suddenly tensed in his seat and pointed toward the museum. "That--"

Casper looked out the window and appeared curious. Hayes walked with Riley down the four steps from the museum and guided her toward his nearby car in no apparent hurry. Despite the earlier incident with the scaffolding, he appeared particularly jovial that evening. Riley, on the other hand, looked distracted.

"Why don't we grab something to eat before I take you home?" Hayes suggested while smiling at her.

"Not tonight," she announced, not sharing his good mood. "It's been a long day."

Hayes stopped by the passenger side door and turned to face her. He was obviously very sensitive to her moods and felt the need to fix things.

"Is everything okay? Are you sure you weren't injured when you fell?" he asked and again visually inspected her for injuries. "I could run you to the emergency room--"

"No, I'm fine," she announced but had a hard time smiling. "My mood has nothing to do with the scaffolding."

"So what's wrong?" he asked. "Did someone say something to upset you?"

"Nothing I can't handle," she replied while frowning. "I just want a hot bath and some pleasant dreams."

"I understand," Hayes replied gently then smiled warmly. "Just not too long in the tub, I tend to get pruney."

Riley stared at him then smiled and laughed softly. "You're a terrible flirt--and I really mean *terrible*."

Hayes opened the door for her while grinning. "We all have our weaknesses, Riley," he announced cheerfully. "I'm happy to say you're mine."

Riley's mood lightened, and she laughed as she got into the passenger side of the car. Hayes shut the door and hurried to the driver's side. Kane and Casper watched from inside the Mustang as Hayes' car pulled away from the museum. Kane was suddenly anxious and kept his eyes on the car. Casper appeared bewildered and a little more than curious.

"Follow them but keep a low profile," Kane said firmly.

"Dude, my profile is always low," Casper announced while grinning.

Casper put the car into drive and followed Hayes' car from a safe distance.

†

The small residential neighborhood was quiet with cozy homes lined along the clean, wide street. The house belonging to

Riley's parent was a single-story home with a well-kept yard and the stereotypical, white picket fence. Hayes' car pulled up to the house. As Hayes jumped out and rounded the car to open her door, Riley was already opening her door and exiting the car. Hayes appeared disappointed. She gave him a scolding look.

"You need to stop being such a gentleman and act like my boss for a change," she bluntly informed him. "I can open my own car door."

"Just because you could that doesn't mean you should," he teased.

Riley rolled her eyes while attempting to keep from laughing. Hayes was nothing if not persistent. Her lightened mood seemed to please him. His mood then turned more serious.

"You were quiet the entire ride home," Hayes announced. "Come on. Tell me. What's bothering you?"

"Nothing you want to know about," she replied.

"Oh," he said with a disappointed sigh and casually folded his arms across his chest. "Is it because of Randy today? You're still mad that I fired him, aren't you?" Hayes stood firm and appeared unwilling to back down. There would be no reasoning with him on his decision to fire Randy. "You realize that wasn't just about you, Riley."

"No, I understand why you had to fire him," she replied. "It's not about Randy."

"It's Chrissie and Jillian and their gossiping, isn't it?" he suddenly deducted then frowned as his arms fell to his sides. "It's my fault people gossip like that about us. I should consider your reputation before acting the way I do."

"You mean the rumors that we're having an affair?" Riley asked with surprise then snorted a laugh and waved him off. "I can handle that." She appeared tense and fidgeted. "It's just--ever since you promoted me to assistant curator a few months ago, certain people have been treating me like I'm not worthy of the new responsibilities."

"That's ridiculous," Hayes announced. "When it comes to qualifications, you're more qualified for my job than I am. You got your college degree, and that's what got you that promotion. How I feel about you had nothing to do with it. You know that." He was silent a moment then raised his brows. "Anyone at the museum who matters knows that too."

Riley smiled warmly, placed her arms around his neck, and hugged him. Hayes returned the embrace with a little too much enthusiasm and appeared reluctant to release her. She laughed softly while tearing herself from his arms. Hayes grinned and hid his embarrassment.

"Although, because of how I feel about you," he casually announced and attempted to hide his smile, "I would be willing to fire anyone who's bothering you."

Riley laughed softly and patted his chest. "It's noble the way you defend me, Hayes, but I'm a big girl. I can fight my own battles."

"Yes, I'm positive you can," he replied. "I realize I'm not much of a warrior, but I'm perfectly willing to fight a few of those battles for you. All you have to do is ask."

"You're sweet," she replied and touched his face. "If that day ever comes, I'll be sure to let you know."

Hayes obviously enjoyed her hand on his face and possibly refrained from moaning. She stared into his eyes with an almost strange look, removed her hand, and immediately tensed. She forced a tiny smile.

"I'll see you in the morning," she said gently.

"Good night, dear."

Riley headed for the house while Hayes watched her from alongside his car. Once she was safely inside, he returned to the driver's side and drove away. The Mustang was parked just down the road from the house. Casper eyed the house from within the car then looked at Kane, who stared transfixed at the house. He couldn't seem to tear his eyes away from the little house.

"Who is she? She's hot," Casper announced.

"That's the bitch who murdered Selena," Kane growled while digging his fingernails into the car door.

Casper stared at Kane with a bewildered look then suddenly appeared horrified. "I don't know what's going through your head, but whatever it is, stop it. That girl didn't kill Selena. She didn't kill anyone."

"No, but she's going to."

"Friend or not, if you're thinking about harming that girl, I'm going to put a serious hurting on you."

He turned on his seat and glared at Casper with a frightening look in his eyes. "She murdered Selena!"

"Yeah, five years from now!" Casper lashed back and now seemed horrified at Kane's psychotic state of mind. "That girl is an innocent kid possibly under the legal drinking age. She hasn't hurt anyone, and if you even think about harming her, you're the monster."

"It's the only way, Casper! Selena's dating Tucker. I never knew they even dated," Kane lashed back. "There's no way I'm going to get her away from him and out of town in one week! I need the radical solution. I kill Riley and Selena lives. It's my call, and I'm making it."

Casper removed his cell phone and placed his finger on one of the buttons. "Then I'll be making my own call, dude. What's it going to be?"

They stared at one another in a long, awkward silence. Neither man flinched. Casper was serious, possibly for the first time in his life. Friend or not, he wasn't going to allow Kane to commit murder. Kane sneered at him and appeared defeated.

"Fine," he growled. "You win, but you'd better come up with another way to keep that bitch from killing Selena."

"Yeah, sure, dude," Casper announced with relief as his large body sagged. "I'll think of something. Let's grab something to eat and chill out at my place."

Chapter Ten

Casper sat in the corner of the sofa with a bottle of beer in his hand and a bag of cheese curls on his lap. Several empty containers of Chinese take-out lie scattered across the coffee table. The new containers were difficult to tell from the old ones. A smell test was the best method to distinguish the two. Kane attempted to relax on the teetering chaise with his own bottle of beer and appeared deep in thought. Casper watched him a long moment in near silence then finally spoke.

"We'll save her, dude. I promise," Casper announced gently while appearing overly relaxed then lazily ate another cheese curl from the bag. Half a dozen more were scattered on the sofa alongside him.

"I know," Kane said softly. "We have to. There's no room for failure on this one."

Casper seemed curious while staring at Kane. "What happened to Nana?" he finally asked. "I mean, she's as healthy as a horse. We just had dinner at her house last Sunday. How is it possible she dies in less than three years?"

Kane glared at Casper with raised brows. "I thought I wasn't supposed to tell you too much about our future? Wasn't that your rule?"

"It's Nana," Casper whined softly. "I never knew either of my grandmothers. She's the only one I've got. I mean, where will I ever get good cooking like that again? Sorry, Kane, your mother is no Nana."

"Careful, it's Nana's good cooking that did her in," Kane informed him then sighed deeply giving in to Casper's question. "It happened very fast, and the doctor said she didn't suffer. I guess she had too much excitement on her birthday." There was an odd silence. Kane grinned and shook his head. "But she really wanted that stripper."

Casper grinned and chuckled. "Oh, Nana," he teased while struggling to keep his eyes open. "She's a wild one."

"Sometime after I dropped her off at home that evening, she had a massive heart attack," Kane said gently. "That was it. Just like that; she was gone."

"Poor Nana," Casper said softly as his eyes shut.

Casper slept peacefully in the corner of the sofa with a cheese curl in his hand and two on his chest. Kane approached Casper on the sofa, stood over him with a curious look, and gently nudged his shoulder.

"Casper?"

There was no response. He was out. Kane removed a bottle of sleeping pills from his pocket and casually tossed them into the garbage. He grabbed Casper's car keys from the counter and left the apartment.

✝

Carl and Naomi Jericho sat on the sofa together in the living room of the charming home while watching the television program's ending credits. Carl finally turned off the television and stood wearily while stiffly stretching. Naomi collected her empty teacup and joined him.

"That show just isn't the same without Riley's commentary," Carl announced then glanced at his wife. "Is she feeling okay? She went to bed early."

"Just some trouble at work again. There's been a lot of pressure with her promotion," Naomi replied.

"She's dating her boss," he remarked casually. "How much pressure could she really have?"

Naomi appeared surprised and mildly offended by his comment. "She's not dating her boss, Carl," she scoffed. "You're such a gossip whore."

"I'm a whore, huh?" he asked while grinning deviously. "You just gave me a really good excuse to jump on you."

Naomi playfully screamed and ran down the hall as Carl chased after her. They could be heard giggling all the way down the hallway. The sound faded as their bedroom door closed. A moment passed. There was a faint scratching at the front door as the knob jiggled. The door slowly opened to reveal Kane. He looked around the dimly lit living room then quietly entered and gently shut the door behind him.

A gentle breeze blew through Riley's open bedroom window while blowing the sheer curtains inward. Riley slept peacefully beneath the covers. Kane stood over her with a hunting knife clutched in his gloved hand and stared at her while she slept. She wore a low-cut tank top, which revealed her ample cleavage, and her arm was draped across a stuffed animal on the bed. She had a childlike innocence about her while sleeping. Kane shut his eyes and lowered the knife. He didn't doubt she was dreaming about kittens and puppies. Casper was right; she was innocent. This wasn't the monster that killed Selena. There was no possible way he could commit cold-blooded murder--not even to save Selena. Despite having made the right decision, he was disappointed with himself. Riley slowly woke and wearily looked across the room. There was no one there. She stared at the open window a moment and watched the curtains flutter with a bewildered expression.

Kane hurried across the lawn and away from the house with his hands deep in his pockets. He quickly approached the Mustang parked across the street and leaned on the car while holding his head. His emotions were again on a roller coaster. He couldn't do what needed to be done. He would have to find some other way to save Selena from being killed. Someone moved in the shadows near the house. Kane uncertainly looked at the house and stared into the shadows. Nothing moved. He then looked at Riley's bedroom window. It was now closed.

✝

Hayes Dante's large, stone house was lavish and impressive by almost every standard. The two-story home was located in a quiet, influential neighborhood surrounded by other equally expensive homes. Hayes was a man of wealth long before he accepted the position of museum curator. He came from a wealthy family and attended an Ivy League college, earning his PhD in Anthropology. He had spent most of his life earning his degrees, studying his field, and doing years of research and exploration. His life was all about his work, and he took his work very seriously. That almost all changed overnight when he met Riley. With all his study and all his learned knowledge, an awkward teenage girl was suddenly showing him up. From the moment he'd met the fifteen-year-old know-it-all with an eidetic memory, he knew he hated her. It was an insult to have to mentor her. She got under his skin every day and in every way. What probably bugged him most was when he realized she was smarter than he was. What gradually turned into a deep routed respect, quickly spun off into him talking the museum into using thousands in grant money to put the young, know-it-all through college. What the museum didn't cover, he made up with his own money. He believed in Riley's abilities and wanted to see her succeed, even if it meant she'd find a better job elsewhere. That wasn't the case. He'd set her free and she returned to him. He had little intention of ever letting her go again.

Hayes slept beneath the covers on his king-sized bed and appeared restless. His massive master bedroom was as impressive as the rest of his house. Double French doors led to the balcony. There were built in bookcases surrounding a large, stone fireplace. The room was incredibly neat and tidy for a single man. His was a sad, lonely existence with no one to share his life. Oddly enough, before he had met Riley, he never realized just how sad and lonely he actually was. A gentle breeze blew past him. He slowly woke and looked to the open French doors. Hayes suddenly appeared concerned and bolted upright in bed. A shadow loomed over him. Hayes looked alongside him and gasped with surprise.

✝

*K*ane quietly slipped into Casper's dimly lit apartment with the borrowed car keys in his hand. He gently shut the door behind him, locked it, and set the keys on the kitchen table. The living room light suddenly came on. Kane looked across the room to where Casper now sat on the sagging sofa. The look of betrayal and anger chiseled onto Casper's face was almost frightening. Kane straightened and attempted to talk his way out of the lecture that was sure to follow.

"I, uh, couldn't sleep, so I took a walk," Kane announced with some uncertainty.

Casper's expression didn't change. He held up the bottle of sleeping pills and gave them a firm shake. Kane stared at the bottle he had thrown in the trash. No amount of lying would get him out of that one. Casper lunged up from the sofa. Despite his large frame, he was amazingly agile.

"What did you do?" Casper demanded.

"Nothing, I swear."

Casper took two quick steps toward him and thrust his palms into Kane's chest, sending him roughly into the kitchen table. Casper's look was nearly psychotic.

"What did you do?" he shouted with conviction.

Kane half lie on the table and stared at his usually even-tempered friend. Casper's aggressiveness was almost frightening. He had never seen him like this before and certainly not directed at him. Kane feared moving from the table.

"Nothing, I swear," Kane quickly announced. "I went to her house, but I couldn't bring myself to harm her. You were right, okay? She's just an innocent girl."

Casper backed away from him and shook his head with disgust. "I considered reporting my car stolen. I even considered placing an anonymous call to the police to check out her house," he growled. "You have no idea how lucky you are that I didn't do either of those. I've known you most of my life, and I just couldn't bring myself to believe you'd do something so sinister and evil." Casper's hostility didn't diminish any. "But know this; if I had been wrong, and you did anything to harm that girl, I wouldn't hesitate to put you in the ground."

Kane slowly moved off the table and sheepishly straightened. He'd never seen his friend that angry. He wouldn't believe Casper capable of harming anyone, but he somehow knew his threat wasn't an empty one.

"She was holding a stuffed animal," Kane said softly and couldn't look at his angry friend.

Casper stared at him a moment and appeared bewildered. "What?"

Kane lowered his head, raked his fingers through his hair, and sighed softly. "She was sleeping with a stuffed animal in her arms," he informed him gently. "What the hell happened to her after Hayes died?"

Casper groaned softly as his mood softened. He leaned against the table near Kane. "The man she respected and admired was killed in front of her, and she was left emotionally and physically scarred.

Revenge is a powerful motivator, Kane." He gave him a stern look. "It almost drove you to murder."

"What are we going to do?" he asked softly.

Casper stared at him with all seriousness. "I'll tell you what we're going to do," he firmly announced. "We're going to stop Hayes from dying."

Chapter Eleven

$\mathcal{T}$he museum had even more buses and children running around outside that following morning. As the groups of children got younger, the noise level and chaos grew louder. Several frazzled teachers and chaperones appeared unable to control the massive swarm of children taking over the sidewalks. Little girls chased little boys in what appeared to be the great 'cooties' crusade. Sadly, the boys were losing. Casper's Mustang pulled up to the museum not far from the main entrance. Casper glared at Kane, who sat silently sulking in the passenger seat. Kane looked ashamed and was unable to make eye contact with his obviously irritated friend.

"Okay, this is it. I'm giving you just one more chance," Casper informed him in a low, harsh tone. "I don't know who you are, but you'd better know I'm serious when I say that I'm two seconds away from running over your ass."

"I know," Kane said softly and stared at the dashboard. "I'm sorry."

"You better be sorry," Casper snapped. "Friends don't drug friends, take their beloved cars out for a joyride, and put scratches on the paint. This car is my baby." His look was stern and serious.

"I didn't mean to--"

"Acht," Casper snapped while wagging his finger at him. "The wound is too fresh. Don't even go there."

Kane kept his head down and nodded in response.

"I don't need you," Casper informed him. "I have another one just like you waiting to chew me out for being late again. He's my best friend--not you. Are we clear?"

"Yes, we're clear."

"And if anything happens to that hot girl's ass, I'm taking you down," Casper informed him sternly. "I've taken you down before, and I'm not afraid to do it again."

"I have no intentions on touching her, I swear," Kane said timidly. "I don't even want to talk to her. I'd like to avoid her as much as possible."

"Keep it that way. Now you go in there and become Hayes Dante's new best friend. We know how, when, and where he dies," he announced. "You keep him from dying; Riley doesn't kill Selena." Casper's look was stern and almost threatening. "Now get out of my car. I have to go to work and somehow tell *you* that I can't go out drinking with you tonight, because in the future you're a back-stabbing cocksucker."

Kane sheepishly got out of the car. As he looked back, Casper's Mustang burned out and raced down the road. A few of the kids marveled at the sound and appeared excited to watch. Kane frowned and headed into the museum behind the swarm of children. He entered the lobby and approached the desk while attempting to avoid the hordes of kids running around. Chrissie, Riley, Tucker, and Selena stood around the desk and appeared to be in the middle of some sort of crisis, although that seemed typical during the early morning pre-school rush. Riley was on the phone and appeared concerned.

"He always picks me up on time," Riley informed them while clinging to the phone at the front desk. "I've never known him to be late."

"Maybe I should drive by his place and see if he's there," Tucker suggested.

"Would you?" Riley asked and appeared pleased with the suggestion.

Selena seemed sympathetic as Riley listened on the desk phone. Hayes' voicemail picked up. Riley slammed the phone down with disgust.

"He's not answering," Riley announced. "I keep getting his voicemail."

Tucker passed Kane while heading for the front doors. Kane approached Selena and paused before her. He was so happy to see her but attempted to act casual despite his anxiety about finally talking to her. He was close enough to touch her, and when she looked at him, he couldn't believe how good it felt to make eye contact with her. Now he just needed to make a good first impression.

"Excuse me; I'm looking for Hayes Dante," Kane said politely while attempting his best charming smile.

Selena looked at him and sharply raised her brows. "Take a number," she scoffed then ran after Tucker.

Kane was momentarily stunned by the aggressive brush-off he'd received and helplessly watched as Selena stormed off. What the hell had just happened? Their first official meeting was a disaster! Riley shook her head with disgust, quickly approached Kane, and smiled apologetically.

"You have to forgive Selena," Riley said gently. "We're all a little stressed. Mr. Dante didn't show up this morning. I'm his assistant, Riley. May I help you?"

Kane attempted to remain polite, but given the circumstances, he wasn't sure how long that would last. He didn't want to talk to her. He didn't even want to be in the same room as Riley. "Uh, no. It can wait--"

"Hayes!" Selena cried out.

Riley looked across the lobby to the front door. Hayes hurried into the museum looking distracted and flustered. Riley ran toward him and appeared concerned.

"What happened? We were worried something bad had happened to you," Riley said.

Hayes took her hand in his but appeared unable to look at her. "I'm sorry about not picking you up this morning, Riley. It's just--I had a really bad night. I must be coming down with something," he announced timidly, but it was obvious something had him visibly shaken. "I'll be in my office."

Riley stared at him and appeared concerned about his physical appearance. "Yes, of course," she said gently. "Did you want me to bring you some tea?"

Hayes finally looked at her, managed a tiny smile, and nodded his appreciation. "Thank you, Riley," he said gently. "Give me an hour, okay?"

Riley nodded although she clearly wanted answers. Hayes hurried across the museum lobby toward the back corridor containing the offices. Chrissie, Riley, and Kane stared after him with equally bewildered looks.

"Talk about acting strange," Chrissie muttered.

Selena and Tucker now joined them at the desk. Selena leaned on Riley's shoulder and stared after Hayes as he disappeared into the connecting corridor.

"What's with him?" Selena asked. "He looked as if the devil himself was chasing him."

"I honestly don't know," Riley replied softly while shaking her head.

"I'm thinking our esteemed boss had a bad trip last night," Tucker remarked with a soft chuckle.

Chrissie laughed softly. Selena moved away from Riley and cast a stern look at both Tucker and Chrissie. Riley's look was disapproving as well.

"He's a little too straight to be doing drugs," Selena informed them.

"It's a funny image though," Chrissie giggled.

"He's not on drugs," Riley snapped and appeared irritated by the entire conversation. She glanced at Kane then glared at the others. "And you should know better than to say such things in front of visitors."

Chrissie rolled her eyes and minded the desk. Tucker turned toward Chrissie. Whatever he did or gestured made her laugh. Selena and Riley glared at both with distaste.

"Knock it off, both of you," Selena snapped, catching both by surprise.

Chrissie returned to sorting brochures. Tucker was quick to leave the front desk. Selena had successfully chased them away without even trying.

"Maybe I should come back later," Kane finally announced. It seemed like a bad time, and he doubted his visit would accomplish anything this morning.

Riley immediately turned toward him and smiled pleasantly. "Oh, I'm so sorry, uh, I didn't catch your name."

"It's Kane."

"I'm sorry, Mr. Kane," she announced gently. "This is a very unusual situation. If you'd be willing to hang out for an hour, I'm sure Mr. Dante will see you."

Kane didn't know if he wanted to hang around for an hour and tolerate Riley's company. He was about to respond when Riley continued.

"Perhaps Selena could give you a tour of the museum while you wait," Riley suggested.

Kane hesitated then glanced at Selena, who now looked at him and smiled. His heart pounded in his chest to the suggestion--or was it her smile? Either way, he'd finally get some time alone with her.

"I'd like that," he heard himself respond.

Kane hoped he hadn't sounded too eager, but the words just slipped out. Selena smiled and extended her hand across the lobby. Perhaps things weren't as bad as he initially thought.

Chapter Twelve

*N*early an hour had passed as Kane walked alongside Selena at a leisurely pace through the North American exhibit. He couldn't help but watch her and smiled as she talked about the exhibits with great knowledge. After all he'd been through the last four days, he finally felt whole again. For a brief moment, nothing else seemed to matter. He fought the urge to come on strong, even though his instincts were screaming for him to seduce her right there. Every erotic memory of her flooded his mind, making it hard to concentrate. For the moment though, he was happy just walking alongside her.

"Your knowledge and enthusiasm for your work is astounding," he announced warmly and laid on the charm. "How long have you worked here?"

"A little over a year," she replied. "Technically, I'm still a trainee."

"I'm sure in a few years you'll be running this place," he informed her cheerfully.

Selena smiled and appeared humored by his compliment. "I appreciate that, but Riley has seniority over me."

"Really? Is she even out of high school?"

Selena laughed softly. "She graduated college last year, but she's been working here since before the dinosaurs arrived," she informed him.

They heard raised voices across the exhibit. Selena was immediately interested and nudged him closer. Jillian, Collin, and Noble stood near a replica of 'Kitty Hawk'. Noble was ranting loudly despite Collin's attempt to get him to keep his voice down. Something obviously had him irritated. Selena glanced at Kane and flashed a knowing smile.

"That's Noble, our P.R. guy," she informed him. "Apparently there was a screw up with the fliers for the fundraiser this Friday night. It's sort of a big deal. Like the super bowl of museum fundraisers. Completely sold out. Noble is real good at blaming others for his mistakes." She appeared to sink into thought. "At least he can't blame me this time."

"Is that why we're pretending we're not listening?" Kane asked while hiding his smile.

Kane had been through this exact situation many times before with Selena. Noble had a bad reputation for blaming her and others. She often complained about his inability to do his own job. Kane was actually surprised the guy kept his job long enough for him to meet him in the future.

"I'm not the type to eavesdrop. I'm just making sure he doesn't attempt to blame me," she informed him. Despite her reassurances, it was obvious she'd listened in on their conversations before. "That man he's talking to; that's Collin. He's one of our top restorers. He was actually up for museum curator, but they hired Hayes instead. Was he ever pissed."

Kane was familiar with her future boss, Collin. According to Selena; Collin was demanding and delegated a lot of his work onto her. He wasn't curator material, but apparently, after Hayes' death, he somehow secured the position. He wasn't a bad worker; he just lacked organization and diplomacy.

"Collin would make a terrible curator, in my opinion," she casually informed Kane. "He's terribly unorganized, and he has zero diplomacy."

At least that sounded like the Selena he knew.

"Who the hell does he think he is?" Noble demanded in a louder than necessary tone. "I told him I'd take care of it. It's my job, and I think I can handle making the necessary corrections. He's making me look bad."

"Is it fixed?" Collin asked.

"His little sidekick took it upon herself to make the corrections," Noble snapped. "I'm getting a little tired of being shown up by that girl."

"Since when is it her business to do your job for you?" Jillian demanded with a huff while folding her arms across her chest. "She's got to have her fingers in everything."

"If I were curator, the first thing I'd do is get rid of Riley," Collin announced.

Noble snorted a laugh at the comment. "Sure you would," he remarked. "If you were curator, she'd be sleeping with you instead of Hayes."

"As pleasant a thought that might be, I'd have to turn her down," Collin remarked firmly. "I'd run this place the way it should be run. I wouldn't want Riley attempting to push her will on all my decisions the way she does with Hayes. He's such a pushover when it comes to her."

"They never should have hired Hayes over you anyway," Noble remarked. "I don't know what they were thinking--hiring an outsider like that."

"He had a reputation," Collin snorted. "Just because the guy had the means to travel the world--"

Selena led Kane away and shook her head with disgust by the conversation they'd witnessed.

"I couldn't imagine Collin as curator," she announced firmly. "I'd feel sorry for his assistant. Hayes is a great curator. I heard he was a little rough around the edges in the beginning, but he's mellowed considerably over the years."

"Your co-workers don't seem to have a favorable opinion of him," Kane remarked.

"They're just jealous of him," she insisted. "Those who don't do their jobs don't like Hayes. He doesn't tolerate laziness and incompetence. That's probably why we get along so well." She obviously had a special fondness for her boss and his abilities. "Trust me; this place couldn't function without him."

Kane couldn't help but wonder what the future would hold if he successfully altered future events. If Hayes didn't die, Riley would probably continue as his assistant in the position Selena was working when he met her. He hoped that small change of events wouldn't alter their eventual meeting in three years. Of course, now that they'd already met, had he already changed future events? It was a sobering thought that made his head hurt. He decided it didn't matter. As long as he kept Selena from dying, he'd accept whatever new reality fate provided.

"So what do you do, Kane?" she asked with a tiny smile and a curious tilt of her head.

"I own an antique store--" He pointed then hesitated. He couldn't admit to owning the antique store in town, since he technically didn't yet, and he certainly couldn't risk her showing up there and running into his 'other' self. "--in the city."

"You and Hayes should have a lot to talk about then. He's into that."

He was a little surprised by her comment. She didn't even seem interested. "You don't care for antiques?"

She groaned softly. "I'm around them all day. The last thing I want to see when I leave here are old things and kids," she remarked then grinned and leaned closer to him. "FYI, the definition of trainee is 'she who cleans up vomit'."

"I can see your point," he replied although he actually didn't. Now seemed like the perfect opportunity to secure a date with her, and he knew exactly what she liked. "You might enjoy that comedy club in the city. Definitely no kids there."

"The dance clubs are more my thing," she informed him without hesitation. "Scarcely a soul over thirty." She looked at him and immediately appeared embarrassed by her comment. She smiled timidly. "No offense."

Kane was a little surprised but somehow managed a smile. "None taken." He couldn't deny the comment regarding his age stung a little.

Chapter Thirteen

*K*ane sat on one of the lobby benches with his head against the wall and watched children run around. Their deafening screams echoing off the tall ceiling didn't even faze him. He was off in his own world, the world where Selena was still alive, and his biggest concern was what colored napkin would match the bridesmaids' dresses. Casper approached, studied him a moment, and then sat alongside him.

"What happened? You sounded strange when you called," Casper remarked.

Kane groaned as he sat up then immediately hunched over with his hands clasped between his knees. "She thinks I'm old," he muttered softly.

"Well, you do have an additional five years on her," Casper informed him.

"She thinks thirty is old, so that must make me ancient," he scoffed. He fidgeted and shifted on the bench. "It's not just the age thing. I don't know what happened. When we first dated, she was fascinated that I worked in my family's antique store. I tell her I *own* a shop and nothing. To make matters worse; every weekend for months, she'd drag me to that comedy club in the city, but now she has no interest in it." He looked at Casper and shook his head with defeat. "How am I going to win her over if she keeps changing the rules?"

"You're being too hard on yourself, dude," Casper announced and patted his shoulder. "You don't even meet her for another three years. She probably did a lot of growing. Besides, that's not what's important right now."

"It's important to me," Kane muttered.

"Then you'll just have to stick with it," Casper said and smacked his thigh. "Whatever made her fall in love with you in the future will eventually kick in."

"Unfortunately, I don't have that kind of time." Kane then muttered, "I wish I told her I was twenty-nine."

"Dude, you're no twenty-nine," Casper remarked sternly. "I would know; I just saw you ten minutes ago at twenty-nine." Casper casually glanced across the lobby, saw Riley approaching them, and grinned deviously. "Here comes your girl, Lizzy Borden. God, she is so hot!"

Kane glanced at Riley as she approached and straightened with some discomfort. He muttered to Casper, "I swear, if you say that one more time, I'll hit you."

Casper wasn't wrong though. Riley was an undeniably attractive, young woman. If Kane hadn't wanted to kill her so badly, he'd probably think so too.

Riley paused before their bench and smiled pleasantly at Kane. "I'm sorry that took so long, Kane," she announced. "Mr. Dante will be out in a few minutes."

Casper grinned at Riley then smacked Kane's thigh, jolting him out of his death lock stare at the young woman. Kane glared at Casper, who shifted his eyes repeatedly at Riley. Kane rolled his eyes then looked at Riley and attempted to sound polite.

"Miss Jericho, this is my associate and former friend, Casper," Kane muttered with disinterest. "Casper, this is Riley Jericho, Hayes Dante's assistant."

Casper stood and politely shook her hand. "It's a pleasure to meet you, Miss Jericho."

"Please, call me Riley."

"I certainly will," Casper replied with a lustful grin across his face.

"Down boy," Kane growled.

"You have to forgive Kane. He's not himself these days," Casper said while giving Kane a devious look.

"There's a lot of that going around," Riley replied with a defeated sigh as she glanced across the lobby at Hayes as he approached. She shifted her attention to Casper, who still stood before her. "Did you want to grab some coffee while you wait for your associate?"

"I never turn down caffeine or pretty ladies."

Kane glared his displeasure at Casper. Casper raised his brows suggestively to Kane, linked Riley's arm to his, and proudly walked away with her. Kane stood as Hayes approached. Both men shook hands.

"What do I owe today's visit, Mr. Kane?" Hayes said and appeared more like his old self.

"Actually, that's first name Kane," Kane corrected. "My business associate and I were invited on a dig in New Mexico with Dr. Grant Melbourne--"

"*The* Dr. Melbourne?" Hayes suddenly asked then grinned. "I think I'm about to be insanely jealous."

"He was my college professor," Kane informed him. "I'd heard about your benefit this Friday and mentioned it to Dr. Melbourne. His schedule is wide open."

Hayes appeared stunned while staring at him. "Dr. Melbourne is willing to come to our benefit?"

"He said he'd be delighted to attend and is looking forward to meeting you. He's expecting your call." Kane removed a card from his pocket and handed it to Hayes.

"I'm--stunned. This is an amazing honor. Did you know every one of his four siblings have doctorates? His youngest sister wrote this amazing book--" Hayes stopped himself from rambling then grinned. "You must really feel bad about that coffee business yesterday."

"Actually, I was interested in attending the benefit but was told it was sold out."

"I'll get you special VIP passes," Hayes announced without hesitation then laughed. "Hell, I'll even give you Riley for the evening."

"That's not necessary," Kane muttered.

Kane's eyes strayed past Hayes to Selena across the lobby. He stared longer than he should, but he couldn't help himself. Hayes followed his stare then grinned.

"Oh, I see," Hayes said with a chuckle. "You're the adventurous type, huh?"

Kane quickly looked at him and appeared surprised. "What? No, you've misjudged me--"

"With all the grants and donations Dr. Melbourne is going to generate, I'll gladly arrange for Selena to be your escort Friday night," Hayes announced while grinning. "In a way, I'm actually relieved. Honestly, I'd be lost at these things without Riley by my side."

Kane fumbled. He knew he should protest, but Selena as his escort was exactly what he wanted. He hated to sound desperate, but he obviously was.

"Are you sure she won't mind?" Kane asked while tensing at the thought of Tucker disapproving.

"No, not at all," Hayes insisted then offered a knowing smile. "You do realize 'escort' means introducing you to the right people. I'm not pimping out my employees."

Kane immediately tensed and felt embarrassed by Hayes' directness. "Rest assured, the thought never crossed my mind," he replied. Actually, that was a lie. Thoughts of Selena in sexually compromising situations seemed to be all he was thinking about lately. "What I meant was; doesn't she have a boyfriend? You know, big burly guy. Kind of intimidating."

Hayes chuckled softly. "Yeah, I've met him," he teased. "I assure you, Tucker isn't invited to Friday's gala. He's not exactly gala material. It's my opinion that some time away from that one will do her a lot of good."

A strange smile crossed Kane's face. Perhaps that was the influencing factor that changed in Selena's life before he met her. "If that's the case," Kane announced, "then I'd be honored if you'd arrange that."

"Consider it done," Hayes announced cheerfully. He grinned and eyed the card in his hand. "Dr. Melbourne at our gala. If you were a woman, I'd kiss you."

"I'd rather you didn't."

Hayes sharply raised his brows. "You apparently missed the 'if' in that statement."

Both exchanged grins and chuckled softly.

Chapter Fourteen

$\mathcal{I}$t was Friday night and the museum gala was already underway. There were limousines parked in front of the museum as lavishly dressed patrons walked the red carpet for the well-publicized gala. It was a huge deal to the museum. The benefit would bring millions in grants for research and upkeep. High society types and anyone of importance from miles around attended the benefit. The crowded lobby contained massive buffet tables and caterers carrying trays of expensive delicacies and crystal glasses of champagne. A small orchestra played classical music, lending elegance to the already high-profile gala. Kane and Casper were among those in attendance and looked equally handsome in their black rented tuxedos. Kane appeared tense awaiting his 'date' and looked around while Casper fiddled with his tie.

"I feel like a penguin trapped in a tuxedo," Casper muttered. He was obviously out of place, even if he looked the part of some wealthy investor.

"Just remember to make yourself scarce," Kane informed him while fidgeting. "I need time alone with Selena."

"You're not exactly alone."

"You know what I mean," Kane muttered. Casper's lack of female companionship sometimes kept him disengaged from the world of love and relationships. Kane wished he had pushed Casper to date more. "Her burley boyfriend wasn't invited, so this is my big chance to spend some quality time with her."

"By quality time; I'm going to assume that doesn't entail getting busy in the restrooms," Casper remarked casually.

Kane glared at his friend. Casper grinned and laughed. He was obviously joking, but Kane wasn't amused. Casper was never going to have an adult relationship with a woman.

"You need to chill, dude," Casper informed him. "I don't remember you being this uptight. I obviously went wrong somewhere. I'd better make a mental note on that."

Hayes approached them with Selena on one arm and Riley on the other. He appeared to be in his glory sandwiched between the two, gorgeous women. Both women wore stunning evening dresses that revealed just enough leg and cleavage to attract attention. Casper eyed Riley and grinned lustfully while raising his brows as he nudged Kane. Kane rolled his eyes at his friend's infatuation with his girlfriend's future murderess. He suddenly remembered why he never pushed Casper to date more. His warped sense of humor and childish behavior around the opposite sex was off-putting to most women. Although Kane couldn't deny Selena looked incredible in her moderately sexy dress, she never actually dressed that way while they dated, particularly to museum fundraisers. Perhaps she dressed a little more provocative prior to their dating or maybe she felt her promotion to assistant curator called for a little less attention to her *asscts*. His eyes strayed to Riley in her moderately sexy dress. Despite being the current assistant curator, she didn't seem to care if her attire turned heads. Perhaps Hayes liked when she dressed that way.

"I'm glad you and your associate could join us tonight," Hayes announced cheerfully.

"Hi, Riley. You look stunning," Casper said with a boyish grin plastered on his face.

Riley smiled at Casper while clinging to Hayes' arm. "You're looking rather sharp yourself, Casper," she announced in a tone that seemed genuine. "Save me a dance?"

"With pleasure," he announced in his most suave voice.

Casper was suddenly reduced to a giddy schoolboy seduced by Riley's feminine wiles. Kane tried hard not to roll his eyes at how easily his friend was swept away by a little leg and strategically placed cleavage. He'd forgotten how horny his friend had been just a few short years ago. Thankfully, he grew out of that phase. Unfortunately, that hadn't happened just yet, and Casper ogling Riley was making him nauseous.

"Selena, this is Kane's business associate, Casper," Hayes introduced them.

Selena smiled and nodded politely at Casper. Casper returned the smile and appeared mentally to undress the attractive woman. Kane wasn't amused.

Hayes then focused his attention on Selena. "Make sure you introduce Kane to all the right people," he informed her. "We want him to make the proper connections."

"I'll be sure to do that," Selena informed her boss.

Selena smiled sweetly and linked onto Kane's arm. Kane stared at Selena longer than he should have. It felt great having her finally touch him. It seemed like a lifetime since he felt her. He had to resist the urge to move too fast. He wanted nothing more than to take her in his arms and make love to her, but he had to stay focused. If he moved too quickly, he'd ruin everything. He'd have to be satisfied with the casual touch.

"Now, if you'll excuse us," Hayes announced cheerfully and affectionately patted Riley's hand on his arm. "Riley's going to make me look good in front of some investors."

Hayes and Riley walked away like museum royalty. She seemed happy to be on his arm, although not nearly as happy as he was to have her there. Soft murmurs were heard from the crowd, which could only mean one thing. Dr. Melbourne had arrived. Dr. Grant Melbourne crossed the room to a whirlwind of chatter and greetings. He was an oddly handsome man in his early fifties. It wasn't just physical attributes that made him appealing to women. He had charm, style, and more charisma than any one man should. His reputation as an explorer was legendary, and Kane and Casper had been lucky enough to have him as their professor in college. Melbourne approached them and chuckled while extending his hand. Casper enthusiastically shook his hand.

"Doc, great to see you again!" Casper said cheerfully.

"Casper," he announced then turned to Kane and shook his hand as well, "Kane." Even men found Dr. Melbourne charming. It was hard to explain his broad appeal. "It's been nearly seven years, hasn't it?"

Kane nodded in response.

Melbourne eyed Kane and appeared slightly humored. "Well, you've certainly put on a few years since college. You're looking a little old there."

Kane frowned at the comment. Now his *old* college professor was calling him old. Melbourne eyed Selena with a glimmer of lust as he briefly scanned her body. She studied him with equal fascination, although it was doubtful she'd fall for his charm. Selena was smarter than Melbourne's usual college groupie.

"Who do we have here?" Melbourne asked while staring at Selena with great interest.

"This is Selena, the assistant curator," Kane announced proudly and subconsciously patted her hand on his arm as he'd done so many times at museum functions in the past--or technically the future.

"Assistant to the assistant," Selena politely corrected and pulled her hand away from his and offered it to Melbourne.

"It's a pleasure either way," Melbourne suavely announced and accepted her hand. He then looked at Kane and grinned without releasing Selena's hand, allowing his thumb gently to caress the top of her hand. "Is this your lovely girlfriend?"

Kane had become accustomed to announcing Selena as his fiancé, so it was challenging to backpedal on their relationship. The way Melbourne held Selena's hand had him slightly distracted, which wasn't helping, and he found it difficult to respond to the question.

"Actually, I guess you could say she's my escort for the evening. You know, introducing me to all the right people." Kane eyed Melbourne's hand still holding Selena's in a sensual manner and tensed at the sight.

Melbourne grinned at Selena while refusing to release her hand. "Trust me, you can do much better," he teased.

Selena giggled. Kane wasn't humored by the comment or Selena's giggle. Melbourne touching her was now particularly disturbing to Kane.

Melbourne looked at Kane and maintained his playful grin. "You don't mind if I steal your date for a dance, do you?" Melbourne asked although he had already pulled her to his side, prepared to whisk her away at a moment's notice.

Kane actually did mind but managed a weak smile regardless. "No, of course not."

Selena allowed Melbourne to steal her away to the dance floor. Both men watched with some surprise as Melbourne danced close with Selena to the slow song.

"Oh, that's cold," Casper announced with a firm shake of his head. "Our old professor stealing your girl--"

"He's not stealing her," Kane corrected a little too firmly. "It's just one dance. Was I supposed to tell him no? Besides, if she thinks I'm old, she must think he's ancient."

Casper stared at the look in Kane's eyes as he watched Selena dancing with Melbourne. "Okay, breathe," Casper snorted then shook his head. "I'd better find us some drinks. You need to mellow."

As Casper headed for the bar, Kane stared at the dance floor and frowned. Melbourne suavely slow danced with Selena and held her close while they talked. It was a little too romantic in nature for his comfort.

"Did your escort ditch you too?" Riley's voice was heard from alongside him.

Kane suddenly looked at Riley standing next to him. He was so caught up in his petty jealousy; he hadn't even seen her approach. He immediately tensed and attempted not to look at her. It was hard for him to loathe the woman with her cleavage staring him in the face.

"I wouldn't say that," he remarked then glanced around the lobby. "What happened to Hayes? I thought he never allowed you from his side at these things."

"He usually doesn't. He saw someone he knew, excused himself, and disappeared without a trace," she announced almost playfully but something about her ridged stance indicated she was bothered. "He's been acting really strange lately." Riley's seriousness quickly faded as she grinned and took Kane's arm. "His loss. How about a dance?"

Being as close as he was to her was emotionally torturing enough. There was absolutely no way he was going to slow dance with the psychopath.

"I don't dance--"

"It's easy. I'll show you."

Riley flashed a grin, took him by the hand, and pulled him to the dance floor. His first instinct was to pull away from her. Her touch cut through him like a knife, but he realized he had to put on a show if he didn't want to attract the wrong kind of attention. As he considered how to get out of dancing with her, he watched Selena dancing slowly and close with Melbourne. Maybe he'd be able to hear some of their conversation if he was closer. He couldn't believe he was actually jealous of Melbourne! Kane turned to Riley on the dance floor not far from Selena, put on his best faux smile, and slow danced with her. She appeared surprised by his dancing style and grinned her pleasure.

"For someone who said he couldn't dance, you're winging it rather nicely," Riley remarked.

"I didn't say I couldn't--just that I don't."

"I'll bet you're a great dipper."

Kane appeared surprised by the comment and actually looked at her for the first time. Before he could question it, Riley spun herself in his arms and gracefully dipped herself. He was slightly stunned by her balance and technique. She pulled herself back up into his arms and danced a little closer. Kane found himself staring at her now. She was a bit unpredictable, in his opinion, which was obviously an understatement. She looked into his eyes and smiled. It was hard not to stare back at her. Her face was burned into his mind from the night she killed Selena, yet now she somehow seemed innocent and incapable of such a brutal act.

"When Selena and I go out to the dance clubs in the city, we compete for the 'most often dipped' title," Riley teased playfully while fixing his jacket lapels.

Her touch disturbed him, but he refrained from reacting. He was more interested in their dance club rivalry. Both looked at Selena and Melbourne, who danced close by. Selena sneered playfully at Riley then said something to Melbourne. He grinned and gracefully dipped her. Riley groaned softly and shook her head while attempting to hide her smile.

"We can beat her," Riley said.

Kane appeared to consider the entire rivalry between them and eyed Selena, who now watched them with her brow playfully raised in challenge. Perhaps he could change the way she saw him by humoring Riley. A devious thought crossed his mind. He spun Riley, pulled her leg up to his hip, and dipped her daringly low. Riley appeared delighted while grinning. He pulled her back up and into his arms, holding her closer than he had intended. Riley laughed and clung to him in an almost seductive manner as her free hand rested on his chest. She stared into his eyes only inches from hers and grinned her approval.

"Now that's how a real man dips."

Kane laughed and for a moment forgot how much he wanted Riley dead. Both looked at Selena and Melbourne while continuing to dance slow and close. Selena said something to Melbourne. He laughed and shook his head. Selena looked at Riley and playfully frowned.

"I'll hold that title for quite some time," Riley informed him cheerfully.

Riley clung to Kane while they continued their slow dance. He was suddenly aware that her hand was still on his chest while dancing excessively close. He'd put himself in a position where he couldn't possibly pull away without looking intentional. Kane uncertainly eyed

Riley in his arms with her head nearly on his shoulder and felt her warm breath against his neck. It sent tingles down his spine. The whole situation was oddly strange. He then looked at Selena dancing with Melbourne only a few feet from them. Selena looked back at him and smiled almost seductively. It was the smile he'd been hoping to see. Kane returned the smile.

Chapter Fifteen

*H*ayes hurried into the lobby while seemingly out of breath and uncertainly straightened his tie. He grabbed a glass of champagne from a passing server and took a large swallow. He scanned the crowded room. His attention immediately focused on Kane and Riley molded together while dancing slow. He stared at them with a perplexed look, frowned, and took another swallow of champagne. A man in his late forties, Albert Mercer, approached Hayes and stared at the dance floor as well.

"You are one lucky man," Albert informed Hayes while watching Riley dance with Kane.

Hayes looked at Albert standing alongside him. Albert was the sort of man most rich people considered wealthy. Nearly all his vacation homes made Hayes' home look like a tin shack. Despite all his millions, he was considered the cheapest donator the museum had ever known. His hand tailored tuxedo and diamond studded watch screamed 'rich guy here'. Despite being a little soft in the middle, he wore his expensive tuxedo well, but he wasn't much to look at above the neck. His bad toupee seemed out of place considering his worth, and he was by no means an attractive man to begin with. He spent too much time on his clothing and jewelry and took little care of his personal hygiene. His eyebrows were excessively bushy for a middle-aged man, and the hair in his ears had grown out further than society standards permitted. The faint smell of body odor was barely noticeable over the excessive amount of expensive cologne he'd bathed in that evening.

"I have few complaints," Hayes announced.

"Dr. Grant Melbourne," Albert said while chuckling. "I don't know how you pulled off that one."

"I have connections," Hayes remarked. "Have you had a chance to speak with Dr. Melbourne?"

"In great length," he replied. "He's very impressed with our little museum."

Hayes seemed to cringe at Mercer's comment. "We've done well for ourselves."

"I think we should talk donations," Albert said cheerfully and placed a hand on Hayes' shoulder. "Dr. Melbourne believes the museum needs to expand. A new wing would bring a lot of needed attention to the museum and our community."

"I agree completely."

"I'm prepared to write a check for one million dollars tonight," Albert announced while grinning at his own generosity.

"That would be most generous, Albert," Hayes informed him while attempting to hold back his enthusiasm. Stroking Albert's ego was unwise and often encouraged added conditions to his perceived generosity.

Albert removed his checkbook from his inner jacket pocket and grinned and he clicked his gold pen. "There is a small matter I'd like to discuss before I write this check."

Hayes tensed but maintained his polite smile. The condition on his generosity was almost certainly about to surface. "Free lifetime admission to the museum? Consider it done."

Albert chuckled and pointed his pen at Hayes while amused. "You're funny, Hayes." He started writing the check and cast a glance at Hayes. "There's this banquet I'm attending tomorrow night, and I'd like Riley to accompany me."

Hayes' entire body suddenly stiffened as he stared at Albert. His expression indicated his thoughts. For a seemingly meek man, the look he gave Mercer was almost frightening. "I'm afraid that isn't possible."

Albert suddenly looked at him and closed his checkbook. "Oh? Why not?"

"I'm sure it's an innocent request, but I would never ask Riley for that sort of favor," he remarked while smiling despite his inability to blink and take his eyes off Albert. His resemblance at that moment to a psychotic serial killer was chilling.

Albert suddenly chuckled, mocking Hayes. Hayes twitched while glaring at him. The look in his eyes didn't change, but Albert was clueless to it.

"You ask her for those sorts of favors all the time," he announced. "Isn't that why she's dancing with Dr. Melbourne's friend?"

"That's different," Hayes remarked and failed at sounding casual. "I brought her here, and I'm taking her home. Technically, she's here with me. I suppose if I attended your banquet that would be acceptable."

Albert's look was stern and serious. "She doesn't need a chaperone, and the whole point of taking her to the banquet would be so that I could take her home."

Hayes didn't take his eyes off Albert. His blue eyes seemingly changed color. "Are you suggesting a condition of your million dollar donation relies on Riley sleeping with you?"

"You're a smart man, Hayes," Albert remarked while grinning. "I shouldn't have to spell it out for you."

"Actually, I think you had to, Albert." Hayes' voice lowered considerably as the words snarled from his mouth. "Because if I'm going to punch you in the mouth, I want to make sure it wasn't just a misunderstanding."

Albert seemed moderately stunned by the comment and finally noticed the look he was receiving. "Do you have any idea how many women would line up for a chance to date someone of my wealth and influence?" he suddenly demanded. "I can have just about any woman I want. It would be to Riley's benefit to cozy up to me." Albert appeared sure of himself and even grinned. "Why don't you ask her?"

"I suppose I could," Hayes replied with little emotion. "But I'm not sure how you'd feel about her ripping your testicles off and shoving them up your ass, which is exactly what you can do with your donation."

Despite Hayes' low, conservative tone, several guests heard the comment and were now staring at them. Albert fidgeted and appeared uncomfortable.

"If you intend to stay, Mr. Mercer, you'll conduct yourself in a proper manner," Hayes remarked sternly. "If not, I'll have security escort you off the premises and you'll never be invited to another one of the museum fundraisers again. Quite frankly, you're a cheap bastard who hasn't given a single dime to our cause. We actually lose money by inviting you, and I'm getting a little tired of you prancing around here acting as if you had anything to do with our success."

More guests now stopped to watch the exchange and talked quietly among themselves. Albert saw the looks he was receiving and appeared even more uncomfortable.

Chapter Sixteen

Later that evening at the museum gala, Selena and Melbourne talked while Kane stood near them with the appearance of a third wheel. He stared at his drink between glares at Selena being charmed by the much older Dr. Melbourne. She laughed at all his jokes, even the bad ones, and occasionally touched his arm in mild flirtation. Casper had stolen Riley away and danced a slow song with her. He appeared to be in his glory while holding her closer than he should have. Riley seemed genuinely interested in his company and kept his attention on her throughout the dance. When Kane looked back, Melbourne was stealing Selena away for another dance as if he wasn't even there. It wasn't the evening with which Kane had hoped. Selena barely knew he existed while in the company of Dr. Melbourne, and he didn't know if there was really anything he could do about it. She technically wasn't his girlfriend. Hayes approached Kane and appeared unusually cheerful.

"Are you enjoying your evening?" Hayes asked.

"Regretting inviting Dr. Melbourne," Kane muttered, took a large swallow of his drink, and maintained his death lock stare on his former professor.

Hayes looked to the dance floor and watched Selena and Melbourne slow dance while unusually close. Selena appeared particularly giddy in his arms. Kane glanced at Hayes as he stared at the couples slow dancing. There was a small blemish on Hayes' neck beneath his shirt collar. Kane appeared curious and attempted to identify it, but Hayes was already looking back at him. Hayes offered a sympathetic smile.

"I'm afraid I can only do so much, but I may be able to help you on your quest for Selena," Hayes announced simply. "We're going to the sticks this week. Some quack survivalist believes he's found ancient treasure. We'll be staying at this romantic bed and breakfast for three nights. If you're willing to hike and get your hands dirty, you're welcome to come along. I promise you, Selena will be bored out of her mind."

Kane stared at Hayes and immediately tensed to the words. As he stared at this man, he was suddenly reminded that Hayes was as much a ghost as Selena. In a matter of days, he would be dead if the past wasn't altered. The ripple effect of his accident was ultimately Selena's murder.

"Hiking, huh?" Kane said and felt a shiver down his spine. This was his opportunity to change Selena's fate and Hayes was just handing it to him. "That's a generous offer."

Hayes snorted a laugh. "Generous is the donation I just received from a wealthy cheapskate because of Dr. Melbourne," he announced. "I owe you."

"I guess it pays to spill coffee on someone," Kane remarked with a snicker.

Hayes grinned in response. Kane found Hayes very likeable and rather interesting. Saving his life suddenly seemed almost as important as saving Selena. Once the song ended, Riley and Casper approached them from the dance floor. She appeared annoyed at Hayes and glared demandingly at him.

"Where the hell were you?" Riley asked.

"Pimping donations," Hayes replied and appeared a little surprised by the harshness of her tone. "You looked like you were enjoying yourself. I didn't want to disturb you."

Riley glared at him with piercing eyes then walked away. Hayes groaned softly and wasted no time hurrying after her. They were oddly reminiscing of an old married couple. Selena approached without Melbourne conspicuously at her side and watched Hayes hurrying across the lobby after Riley.

"What was that about?" Selena asked with a look of surprise.

"I'm going with a lover's spat," Casper replied.

Selena glared at Casper with irritation by the comment. "They're not lovers," she snapped.

"Maybe not, but that was definitely a lover's spat," Casper informed her with a cheap grin.

Selena folded her arms across her chest while glaring at Casper. The hostility was evident in her eyes. "Are you supposed to be the funny one?"

Casper appeared surprised by her tone. Most people found him funny. "Usually, yes, but in this case--"

"Maybe Riley doesn't mind humoring you, but I don't care for you," Selena scoffed lowly and walked away from them.

Both men watched with surprise as she stormed across the lobby and vanished into the crowd. Her reaction seemed oddly off. Kane was painfully aware that Selena had abandoned him, and there was a good chance she wasn't returning.

Casper glanced at Kane with all seriousness. "I have to say, your girlfriend is a bitch."

Kane glared at Casper. He wanted to scold Casper for the remark, but she certainly had come across that way. He wondered what had gotten into her. Riley and Hayes were now seen dancing to a slow song on the dance floor. Obviously, whatever had happened had been ironed out rather quickly. Kane suddenly felt a pang of jealousy as he watched them dance. He was missing the closeness he shared with Selena, and it pained him that he couldn't even touch the woman he loved and had just lost. The longer he watched the couple dance the more unbelievable it seemed that Hayes and Riley could be that close and not be lovers. He decided the rumors about them had to be true.

Casper lightly smacked him on the chest, snapping him out of his self-pity trance. "Let's scope out the buffet," he announced. "I'm starving."

Kane frowned with a defeated sigh and walked with Casper to the massive row of buffet tables. The variety of finger foods was numerous and almost impossible to sample everything offered. Casper took one item from every tray, loading up his plate, and made the impossible a reality. Kane took a carrot stick and played with it rather than eat it.

"What's wrong with me?" Kane finally asked.

Casper cast a glance at him while attempting to balance his loaded plate as he strategically placed more food on it. "Nothing, dude. You're a great catch. You're the right level of easygoing." He cleverly raised a brow and grinned. "Women love a man they can walk all over."

Kane glared at Casper as he stuffed a gourmet cracker into his mouth. Casper caught his glare.

"What?" he asked with his mouth full of cracker that sprayed out when he talked.

Kane rolled his eyes. Casper tried not to laugh. Jillian and Chrissie were at the opposite end of the buffet table and gossiped softly. Despite their lowered voices, Casper easily heard their conversation.

"I wouldn't have believed it if I hadn't heard it for myself," Jillian announced while gasping overdramatically. "Hayes actually threatened Albert Mercer."

Casper suddenly became alert and nudged Kane. He gave a tiny nod to the women at the other end of the buffet table. Kane glanced at Chrissie and Jillian then looked at Casper and raised his shoulders in silent question. Casper secretly indicated the two with his eyes and raised his brows.

Kane rolled his eyes with disgust. "I hate playing charades with you," he muttered.

"Hayes threatened someone named Mercer," Casper informed him softly.

Both now paid attention to the conversation just a few tables away from them.

"What made him threaten Mercer?" Chrissie asked while playing with her empty champagne glass.

"Apparently, he made an indecent proposal involving Riley," Jillian informed her while grinning deviously.

"For the right price, I'd sleep with the pig," Chrissie scoffed while hiding her grin.

"I guess Mercer was so embarrassed because several people heard their conversation, that he gave Hayes a sizeable donation," Jillian remarked and dramatically raised her brows. "I heard it had many zeros."

"Not exactly a brilliant move on Hayes' behalf," Chrissie said with the concern evident in her eyes. "Doesn't he know that guys like Mercer have men killed for less?"

"Might be a blessing in disguise," Jillian said callously. "Maybe then they'd give his job to Collin. He should have gotten the curator job from the start."

"You're only saying that because Collin likes you," Chrissie announced and gave her head a cocky tilt. "Then he'd fire Riley and hire you as his assistant."

"Nothing wrong with that, is there?"

Chrissie considered then shrugged. "No, I suppose not. I've been thinking about cozying up to Collin myself. Even if he's lousy in bed, I'm sure it'd be worth it."

"If you were smart, you'd cut out the middleman and cozy up to Hayes instead," Jillian teased.

She suddenly snorted a laugh and rolled her eyes. "Hayes only has eyes for Riley," Chrissie scoffed while shifting uncomfortably and thumped her empty glass against her palm.

Jillian appeared stunned while staring at her friend. "No way! You didn't, did you?"

Chrissie just frowned.

Jillian laughed while holding her chest. "Oh, my God, you threw yourself at Hayes?" She suddenly became wildly curious and grinned. "What happened? Details, girl!"

Chrissie's face turned several shades of red, and she attempted to avoid the conversation. "What do you think happened? The guy's so dense, I had to practically spell it out for him," she remarked. "Then when I did, he shot me down and threatened my job if I ever came on to him again."

"I'd think you'd learn from the mistakes of others," Jillian teased while attempting to keep from giggling at her friend's obvious embarrassment.

Chrissie rolled her eyes. Both women walked away. Casper looked at Kane and shook his head.

"Your boy isn't exactly popular," Casper remarked. "I'm surprised he lived long enough to have an accident. Sounds like half the employees want to kill the boss."

"Unfortunately, none of this has anything to do with Riley blaming Selena for the accident," Kane remarked then frowned and looked around the lobby. "I need to find Selena and see if I can salvage some of this evening. I can't believe how badly tonight has gone." There wasn't any sign of Selena within the crowded lobby. She successfully vanished. Kane groaned and ran his fingers through his hair with disgust. "Damn it, I don't see her anywhere. You don't suppose she left, do you?"

"I'm sure she's around somewhere," Casper replied then scanned the room as well, paying particular attention to the couples on the dance floor. His brows knitted and a curious look crossed his face. "You know, I haven't seen Dr. Melbourne recently either. You don't suppose the two of them--" Casper grinned and suggestively raised his brows.

Kane glared at him, shifted with discomfort, and sneered. "No, I don't."

Casper chuckled, humored by Kane's jealousy over mention of their old professor and his future girlfriend. "I was just kidding. Relax."

Kane's mind immediately strayed and he considered the possibility. He knew Selena better than that. She wouldn't be star struck with someone like Melbourne. He wasn't even her type. Although, until a few days ago, he didn't think Tucker was her type either. He suddenly had a compelling urge to find Dr. Melbourne.

Chapter Seventeen

*T*he elegant, old country mansion converted into a bed and breakfast was massive and stunning. Nestled within the remote woodlands, the bed and breakfast had an old-world, country charm with some modern flare to attract wealthier clientele. The wraparound porch was broad and inviting with steps on all sides. Nearly every corner of the property was landscaped with flowers, shrubs, and chubby marble cherubs. Casper sat on one of the elegant rocking chairs while Kane paced the length of the porch. Each time he stepped on the same creaking board, Casper grimaced. The stress of Kane's task was starting to weigh on him. His entire mission was coming to a head. If he didn't prevent Hayes' death, he didn't have a backup plan. Well, he did have a backup plan, but Casper wasn't about to let him attempt it. Casper's endless rocking and relaxed state was bothering him more than the nerve-racking wait for Hayes' arrival at the inn.

"Tomorrow is the day it all hits the fan," Casper informed Kane as he lazily rocked in the rocking chair. "You need to get your mind off Selena's ass and focus on keeping Hayes from hiking that trail tomorrow morning."

"I have it covered," Kane replied as he paced. "I'm slipping laxatives into his nightcap."

Casper tilted his head and appeared curious. "Didn't we do that in Boy Scouts?"

Kane flashed a sly grin. "Call me sentimental."

Casper chuckled softly. "Ah, yes, the good old days." He then resumed his seriousness of the situation surrounding them. "Remember how this works," he said firmly.

Kane nodded, stopped his pacing, and stared at Casper. "If I keep Hayes away from that rockslide, he won't die. If he doesn't die, Riley won't have any reason to kill Selena five years from now, and I won't have reason to travel through time. I'll return to the correct time and have no memory of any of this." He continued his pacing but remained tense.

"So stop being so uptight and relax."

He turned toward Casper as every muscle in his body twitched. "I watched her die, Casper. How can I relax? I just want to hold her and tell her I love her, and I can't even do that."

"You will--in three years," Casper announced.

"I don't want to wait three years," he muttered.

"Getting in good with Selena is no longer the goal here," Casper said firmly. "Keep your mind on Hayes. Nothing can happen to him tomorrow. Once you prevent his accident, you're home free." There was a slight pause. "And I can go back to dealing with just one of you. You were really crabby about giving me time off for this little fieldtrip, you know."

"When was I ever crabby about you taking time off?" Kane suddenly asked.

"Seriously?" Casper asked while staring at him. "You hate when I leave you alone with your mother at the store."

Kane grimaced. "Oh, I forgot," he muttered. "The dreaded 'why aren't you married' and 'where are my grandkids' conversations. She was like a broken record." He sighed deeply and sank into thought. "She was so excited when Selena and I got engaged. My mother was finally a joy to be around."

A fairly expensive car drove along the long driveway and approached the inn. Kane and Casper both looked, but the car didn't belong to Hayes. Once the car parked, Noble, Collin, and Chrissie got out of the car and removed their bags from the trunk. Kane and Casper exchanged looks.

"Did Hayes mention others were coming along?" Casper suddenly asked.

"No, he failed to mention that," Kane remarked then quickly brushed it aside. "It doesn't change anything. We'll continue with the plan."

"Just more prying eyes," Casper remarked. "It could make slipping Hayes the laxative a little more complicated."

"I'll think of something," Kane muttered and tried to keep himself from pacing. An alarming thought crossed his mind. "I hope Tucker doesn't show up."

"You said Hayes told you he wasn't invited."

"That doesn't mean he won't show up," Kane muttered and mentally rolled his eyes at the thought.

They approached the porch with their overnight bags and appeared pleased. Collin politely extended his hand to Kane.

"Hayes didn't mention he'd invited you and your associate," Collin announced and immediately looked around with increasing interest. "Is Dr. Melbourne here as well?"

"No, I'm afraid Dr. Melbourne had a lot to do before his upcoming dig in New Mexico," Kane informed him.

There may have been some truth to that. He didn't really know, because he never actually asked. Kane had no intentions of inviting Melbourne along. He didn't need his old, horn dog professor putting the moves on his would-be future girlfriend. It was bad enough his thoughts got the better of him Friday night at the gala when Selena disappeared the rest of the night and no one could find her or Dr. Melbourne. She obviously hadn't hooked up with his old professor. She wasn't the 'one night stand' kind of girl. Yet the incident still made him crazy. He didn't understand his newly found jealousy. He'd never been the jealous type before. He was sure it had to do with Selena's death. It was making him crazy. Not being able to touch her was making him crazy.

"Too bad," Collin remarked and appeared defeated. "I believe you remember Noble and Chrissie from the fundraiser."

Kane and Casper politely nodded to them.

"This is my first work-related fieldtrip," Chrissie announced excitedly while seemingly bouncier than usual. "I was so thrilled that they asked me to come along."

Collin and Chrissie exchanged smirks that the others didn't see but Kane immediately noticed. He was almost certain Collin invited her along for a little fun time in the sack. It seemed odd though. They'd never hooked up before; at least Selena never told him she suspected there had been an affair. Being Chrissie was Selena's best friend, he was positive Selena would have known and told him if that had ever happened.

"Don't be too excited," Noble informed her, lacking her enthusiasm. "Once Riley and Hayes establish that there's something worth our while out there, we're all hiking out to the site and getting our hands dirty."

"I don't mind," Chrissie replied cheerfully. "I'm away from that front desk for a few days."

"We should probably check in," Collin announced and again looked at Chrissie while hiding his lustful smile.

Kane allowed his thoughts to stray. He wondered if Chrissie was given her own room for appearances, or if she was simply shacking up with Collin. If he hadn't been so familiar with these people in the future, he probably wouldn't give their private affairs a second thought. It was actually Selena's fault. She loved sharing work related gossip. It was their evening ritual. His mind once again strayed to Riley and Hayes. Why hadn't Selena ever mentioned either of them? Sure, they were both out of the picture by the time he started dating Selena, but it almost seemed scandalous, so her silence on what happened to them was curious. Of course, she hadn't mentioned she'd dated Tucker either. That was actually something she should have shared with him. Was she embarrassed to tell him that she had dated someone she considered so immoral? He got the distinct impression she never cared for the man, but that obviously wasn't the case. Kane never cared for Tucker. There was just something sleazy about him. Perhaps he felt that way because he had been correct about Tucker having sexual fantasies about Selena. Maybe Kane's instincts about people were better than he thought and that's why he didn't trust the guy. Another car was heard pulling up the long driveway. All five looked at the approaching car. Kane felt his heart pound in his chest then felt disappointment sweep over him. It again wasn't Hayes' car. The expensive BMW pulled up to the inn. Collin and Noble appeared stunned.

"You've got to be kidding me," Collin muttered.

"What?" Chrissie asked.

"It's Mercer," Noble said with a sneer. "Who the hell invited him?"

"This is what happens when the wealthy give large donations," Collin scoffed with the detest showing on his face. "They expect to be able to play weekend archaeologists."

"Didn't I hear Hayes got into it with that guy at the fundraiser?" Kane asked and appeared puzzled. Why would Hayes allow him to come along after what he'd heard happened between them? Large donation aside.

"Some sort of indecent proposal involving Riley," Chrissie informed him while attempting to hide her grin. Sharing that gossip obviously pleased her in some perverse way. "That's a huge no-no. Hayes is very protective over her."

Albert approached the porch while grinning. He wore an expensive suit and shoes to match. He was out of place for the laid-back country inn. A muscular man carried his bags onto the porch behind him. Albert joined them on the porch and grinned while extending his hand to both Noble and Collin. Both men stiffly shook his hand with false smiles plastered on their faces.

"I assume I'm right on time," Albert announced cheerfully to the others.

"We weren't aware you were coming at all," Collin informed him in a halfhearted attempt to sound polite.

"Hayes and I came to an understanding last night," Albert said then looked at Kane and Casper. He smiled and shook both men's hands. "Albert Mercer," he announced cheerfully.

"I'm Kane and this is my associate, Casper," Kane informed him with little interest either way. Although, he'd probably feel differently had the man offered to pay money to sleep with Selena. That would have gotten him punched.

"Oh, yes," Albert chirped. "Friends of Dr. Melbourne. What an amazing man." He then looked behind him and indicated the large, muscular man. "This is my associate, Grier."

Grier barely managed a disinterested nod. He looked like hired muscle more than an associate. Everyone seemed to be thinking the same thing regarding the muscular man. Albert made a face and slapped a bug on his arm. He gave the crushed bug a flick with his thick fingers.

"Hmm, didn't think there'd be so many bugs," Albert announced with distaste and swatted at another. "We'll meet you fellas later for drinks."

Albert entered the inn with Grier following while carrying several bags. Once the door closed, the other men sneered. Noble shook his head.

"You'd swear he's moving in," Noble remarked. "And what's with the hired muscle?"

"This fieldtrip already officially sucks," Collin announced and headed inside.

Noble and Chrissie followed him. Casper and Kane exchanged looks. Something seemed terribly wrong and both men obviously sensed it.

"I have this strange feeling that Mercer guy wasn't among the guests in the original version of this little expedition," Casper remarked.

"I don't know that any of what happened between Mercer and Hayes originally happened before Melbourne attended the fundraiser,"

Kane said with concern and tilted his head. "Do you think it means anything?"

"Nothing that concerns us or our mission, I'm sure," Casper remarked. "Hayes still dies in that rockslide. If he didn't, you wouldn't be here." Despite his words, Casper no longer appeared convinced. "I just can't shake this feeling that I caused a nasty little ripple in the timeline."

"Should we be worried?" Kane suddenly asked while staring at his friend.

Casper appeared deep in thought then looked at Kane and vigorously shook his head. "No, I doubt it," he replied. "Nothing's changed."

A car pulled up to the inn, causing both to look, but it again wasn't Hayes' car. Riley and Selena could be seen within the car. Something didn't seem right. Kane attempted to look calm but found it difficult. So much was riding on tomorrow, and he still couldn't get Selena's lack of interest in him out of his head. Selena and Riley got out of the car. Casper and Kane appeared bewildered as the two women approached. Hayes was supposed to be with them, but for some unknown reason he wasn't. Selena barely acknowledged Casper. Riley smiled at both.

"You guys came up early," Riley said.

"We wanted to get a good parking space," Casper teased playfully.

Riley laughed, pleasing Casper. Selena just rolled her eyes. Kane couldn't be bothered with his friend's attempts to charm Selena's future killer.

"Where's Hayes?" Kane asked, interrupting them.

"Something came up. He'll be along in the morning," Riley said with the irritation evident in her tone.

Kane was momentarily horrified by what she told him. That was going to mess up his entire plan for the evening. Hayes wasn't making saving his life very easy. A thousand different scenarios raced through Kane's mind.

"Let's check in. I want to take a hot bath then find the bar," Selena announced and already appeared bored.

Riley and Selena walked past them and entered the inn. Casper and Kane exchanged concerned looks then followed both women inside. The main lobby of the inn was rustic and lavishly decorated to the point of gaudy. The decorations hanging on the walls and displayed around the room were exquisite, but there were too many of them, giving the room a cluttered feel. Probably the most distracting part of the inn's feel were the laminated signs on every wall and tabletop indicating what guests shouldn't be doing. 'Do not touch'. 'No long-distance phone calls'. 'Keep light on'. 'Keep light off'. 'For decoration only'. 'Do not use'. Guests could spend hours just reading signs telling them what they shouldn't be doing. The check in desk was simple but elegant. Kane was painfully aware that it was neither old nor antique. It wasn't even a good knock-off considering he spotted it from across the lobby.

The innkeeper was an odd woman in her early forties. Bessie was attractive in her own rights, but her overuse of hairspray and make-up gave her the same cluttered feel as the lobby. Her strawberry blonde hair was obviously dyed and in desperate need of a touchup. Her jewelry was large and clunky with many pieces rattling together with her every movement. The jewelry had an antique look about it, but it also wasn't antique. She obviously tried to create an old feel to the inn, but she used newer things only meant to look old. For as much as she'd spent on an old feel to her furniture and decorations, she could have bought the real thing. Casper picked up a beverage coaster off the coffee table, showed it to Kane, and grinned while deviously raising his brows. The coaster read, 'Please use a coaster'. Kane rolled his eyes at Casper's grin. It was obvious Casper and this woman weren't going to get along at all.

Chapter Eighteen

*A*ll nine guests arrived in the dining room around six o'clock that evening for dinner, which was set up buffet style on the faux antique sideboards. Albert appeared baffled by the concept of buffet style dinner. Perhaps he didn't understand how anyone would be comfortable getting their own meal and then sitting down at a large table with many others. Casper loaded up his plate with the starchy, home cooking. He was your basic meat-and-potatoes guy, and there was plenty of it. By the time they got their food and headed for the table, Collin and Chrissie were already on either side of Selena. Kane opted for the seat across the table from her. Casper sat to his left. Riley sat on the other side of Casper and immediately joked with him about their twin plates overflowing with homemade gravy. Riley wasn't shy about her portions either. Albert took the chair on the other side of Riley, which made her slightly uncomfortable. By her reaction, it was almost assumed that Hayes said something to her about Mercer's proposal.

The dinner conversation naturally revolved around the museum and the success of the fundraiser. Albert appeared smug regarding his large donation, although no one even mentioned it. His hired goon, Grier, offered nothing to the conversation and didn't even speak throughout dinner. The overall discomfort regarding Albert's 'assistant' was mutual among the others. Selena and Chrissie did a lot of talking about dance clubs. Kane avoided the subject, fearful his age would again come up in the conversation if he had. Riley talked with Casper throughout most of the meal, and he was eating up the attention. Kane picked at his food and remained mostly quiet, since even his friend found engaging conversation without him. By the time dessert was served, the question finally arose.

"So where is Hayes?" Collin finally asked while looking at Riley for an answer.

"Yeah," Noble announced. "This is his little party. Shouldn't he be here by now?"

Riley appeared mildly disgusted but managed a smile. "He won't be here until tomorrow morning," she announced. "Something came up last minute."

"Really?" Collin remarked as his brows knitted. "This is the sort of thing he lives for. I can't believe he'd be late. It's not like him."

"I'm sure he has a very good reason for being delayed," she replied.

"You mean you don't even know what's keeping him?" Noble asked while attempting to hold back his mocking grin. "That's a first."

"I don't know everything he does," Riley protested. Something was obviously bothering her, and she seemed determined to set everyone straight. "He's my boss; not my husband."

There were several snorts from the table as some attempted to hide their devious grins. Riley appeared offended and glared at her co-workers.

"I'm sorry," Riley suddenly announced boldly with irritation while glaring at her co-workers. "Did I say something funny?"

Her look was enough to cause the entire table to fall silent. There was something almost hostile with her tone and the way she glared at everyone. Kane felt the fear ripple through his body as he was painfully reminded of his encounter with her the night Selena was murdered. Riley tossed her napkin down, stood, and left the dining room. Once she was gone, Chrissie snickered behind her back. Noble attempted not to laugh. Casper picked at his pie while staring at it and frowned. He obviously wasn't pleased about the way they were treating his newly found friend.

"Sounds like Hayes tossed her over for a younger model," Chrissie teased.

"Younger model?" Noble snorted at the comment and held back his laugh. "Where would he find a younger model? On the playground?"

"That's not nice," Selena snapped and appeared irritated. "Hayes and Riley aren't having an affair." She looked at the others around the table. "And you should all be ashamed of yourselves for talking about your boss that way."

The table fell silent to her scolding and everyone minded their dessert. Kane glanced at Selena and smiled to himself. He was proud of her. She was a little less mature then when he meets her in three years, but she had respect for her boss and co-worker. It made him feel good, and he was very proud of her for taking the high road. She was finally beginning to resemble the woman he fell in love with.

Chapter Nineteen

*B*ehind the majestic inn was a large, in-ground pool connecting to an oversized hot tub. There was also a horse stable toward the back edge of the property. Landscaping encompassed nearly the entire backyard and bordered on excessive. Winding brick walkways led to several fishponds with small bridges crossing them and hidden gazebos in several corners. More chubby marble cherubs lurked in every corner. The first few were cute, but the endless parade of naked, marble cherubs bordered on creepy. They looked like little demonic statues preparing to pounce. Casper casually lounged in the hot tub and watched Kane pace the nearby patio with his glass of wine.

"Remember what we discussed?" Casper said firmly, apparently disapproving of his continuous pacing.

"I'm tense," Kane replied.

"You drank an entire bottle of wine; you should be good and mellow," Casper remarked then muttered under his breath, "and possibly drunk."

Riley and Selena appeared on the patio in their pool cover-ups. They talked softly between themselves, although the conversation wasn't loud enough for either man to hear. Neither appeared particularly happy with whatever they discussed. Selena saw the hot tub and became enthusiastic.

"Thank God! A hot tub!" Selena announced with glee and picked up her pace to join them.

"I bribed the innkeeper for a bottle of wine," Kane said to her as they approached.

Casper muttered, "Two--actually."

"Count me in," Selena giggled.

Kane poured a glass of wine for each woman. Selena took both glasses and joined Riley by the hot tub. Kane refilled his own glass and watched them. Riley removed her cover-up to reveal a tasteful bikini that exposed her ample cleavage and her amazingly toned body. Kane and Casper stared with surprise as their mouths hung open. Selena removed her cover-up to reveal a skimpy, string bikini that just about covered her and left little to the imagination. Kane eyed Selena in her 'barely there' bikini then uncertainly looked back at Riley. He was almost ashamed that he indulged in a second peek at the woman he despised.

"Are you joining us, Kane?" Riley asked while tossing her cover-up aside.

His eyes strayed to her buttocks as they tightened when she spun around on the balls of her feet. He felt his body throb in response. "Be right there."

Both women joined Casper in the hot tub. Casper continued to stare at Riley with his mouth hanging open then looked away with embarrassment. Kane drank the entire glass of wine and refilled it before approaching. He needed to concentrate on Selena. He removed his shirt and joined them by the hot tub while wearing his conservative swimsuit. Kane worked out enough to appear toned, although not nearly as muscular as Tucker. He was certain he knew how to get Selena's attention. She had always been impressed with Kane's chest and broad shoulders. This was one area where he was sure he'd finally receive some notice from her. As he joined them in the hot tub, Selena didn't even look at his chest and shoulders. Kane suddenly felt self-conscious. Perhaps it was her muscle-bound boyfriend filling her head. He certainly couldn't compete with Tucker in that area. Kane sipped his wine and sank into mild depression. When they were first dating, it was all he could do to keep her hands off his chest. Now--nothing.

"Can you believe they don't even have televisions in the rooms?" Selena announced while frowning. "What are we supposed to do for the next three evenings?"

Kane wanted to suggest something, but he knew he wouldn't get away with anything perverted. After all, he wasn't Casper. As he cast a glance at his friend, he could see by his raised brow, Casper was dying to say what Kane was thinking. Thankfully, he refrained from speaking.

"I'm good," Riley announced and sipped her wine.

Casper raised his brows, grinned deviously, and clinked his glass to Riley's glass. She returned the smile. Kane wasn't sure what Riley found so amusing, but he was almost certain she was up to something.

"You've been hanging out with Hayes too long," Selena scoffed while rolling her eyes with disgust. "He's turned you into an old woman."

"In that same comparison, what did Tucker turn you into?" Riley snapped in response.

Riley and Selena glared at each other in an awkward silence. Kane and Casper appeared surprised by the friction. Something was definitely brewing between them and it was rapidly coming to the surface.

Casper leaned closer to Kane and muttered, "I think we're going to need more wine."

"What's with you two? I thought you were friends," Kane finally remarked while attempting to smooth things over between them. He was hoping this wasn't the prelude that started the entire downward spiral for revenge.

Selena glanced at Kane and smirked. "Riley's on her broomstick because Hayes is banging some little vixen," she informed him in a tone that mocked Riley. She cast a look at her young friend. "Now she's no longer the center of his universe."

"You're disgusting," Riley scoffed while rolling her eyes. "You and Tucker deserve each other."

"You're just jealous because I have someone and you don't," Selena lashed out.

"Jealous? Of Tucker?" Riley suddenly asked then snorted a laugh. "I don't think so."

Selena was obviously enraged by the comment. "Maybe if you'd gotten around to fucking Hayes, you wouldn't be feeling sorry for yourself and taking it out on me."

Kane was stunned by Selena's comment. "Is that really called for?" he suddenly demanded.

She glared at Kane with hateful eyes. "Sure, go ahead and defend the little princess," she hissed and gave him a disapproving once over. "Everyone always does, but it's not going to help you get between her legs. They're permanently locked."

Riley had the same look in her eyes as that night in the museum when she killed Selena. Casper and Kane were both shocked by Selena's rant. Kane couldn't even believe Selena was suggesting something so perverted as him wanting Riley, but it was her tone and vulgarity that stunned him.

"What is wrong with you?" Kane retorted without even thinking about what he said. This wasn't the woman he knew. "You're behaving like a spoiled little girl throwing a tantrum."

Selena sneered at Kane and jumped out of the hot tub. "Fuck you." She grabbed her towel and stormed off.

Casper stared after Selena with a dumbfounded expression then glanced at Kane, who was equally stunned. "That had to hurt," Casper muttered.

"You didn't have to do that," Riley casually informed him. "I'm a big girl. I can handle Selena."

Kane looked at Riley with surprise by the comment. He couldn't believe she thought he was defending her and had to set her straight. "I wasn't defending you," he snapped. "I just didn't expect her to be that way."

"She wasn't always like that. Tucker made her that way," Riley casually informed him. There was an awkward silence as she stared at him. Her look was serious yet sympathetic. "You're not her type, you know."

Kane stared at her from the comment. What did she know? He and Selena would be getting married in two weeks if Riley hadn't murdered her.

"Excuse me?" he blurted out while attempting not to sound offended by the remark, but in reality he wanted to drown her in the hot tub. Unfortunately, Casper would never allow it. He was already too attached to the witch.

Riley stared at him and remained calm and sympathetic. "I see how you look at her, but unless you're secretly wealthy, I doubt she'll give you a second thought."

"Ouch, that cut to the bone," Casper said softly.

"It's nothing personal," Riley gently informed him. "You're obviously intelligent and handsome, but you're undoubtedly the settle down, get married, and raise a family type. Selena's the last of the party girls."

"How do you know I'm not the party type?" Kane asked defensively. He didn't like this woman telling him about the woman he intended to marry, and he certainly didn't appreciate her telling him what sort of man he was.

"Dude, who are you kidding?" Casper blurted out then turned to Riley, cleverly raised his brows, and gave her a humored smile. "He's serious daddy material."

"I rest my case," Riley replied.

Chrissie, Collin, and Noble walked onto the patio with pool towels in their hands. They saw Riley in the hot tub, talked among themselves, and opted to use the pool instead. Riley glanced at the three then minded her own business. She didn't say it, but she was obviously bothered. Casper caught her look and possibly felt sorry for her.

"Fuck them," Casper said to her.

Riley glanced at him and smiled gently. "I used to think it was just the women who gossiped around the museum, but that's not the case."

"What you do or don't do is none of their business," Casper informed her. "Don't let them bother you."

"I usually don't," she replied then sighed. "It's just been a weird sort of week."

"Yeah, tell me about it," Casper muttered and eyed Kane, who secretly sulked.

Chapter Twenty

Kane sat huddled on one of the Victorian sofas the following morning with a cup of coffee in his hand and a distant look on his face. He looked at the grandfather clock. It was seven o'clock in the morning. Hayes should have been there by now. If he couldn't doctor his morning coffee, he wouldn't be able to stop him from going on that hike. It was all falling apart fast. Unless Hayes didn't show up at all. That would be perfect! Of course, that wasn't going to happen. Nothing he'd done so far would have caused enough of a time ripple to alter the final result. Destiny was still on its destructive course. If it wasn't, Kane would have returned to his correct time, and his torture would finally end. He wanted this entire mess behind him. It was too much for him to endure.

"Come on, Hayes," Kane muttered.

There were footfalls on the stairs followed by Selena's laughter. Kane straightened and looked to the archway. He didn't know what happened last night, but he somehow had to smooth things over between them. This trip was turning into a disaster where Selena was concerned even if Casper insisted their interaction didn't matter. Selena and Tucker entered the lounge while clinging to each other. Kane appeared surprised to see Tucker then became immediately disgusted. He wasn't supposed to be there. He hadn't been invited!

Tucker grabbed her around the waist and nibbled on her neck while she giggled. Kane felt his entire body tense with loathe and jealousy. They'd obviously spent the night together, and he couldn't stand thinking about them rolling around naked together. Tucker kissed her quickly on the lips, smiled lustfully at her, and left through the main door. Kane knew that smile. It was the coveted 'sex was great last night' smile. Seeing that smile on Tucker's face made Kane ill. Selena approached the beverage cart while grinning, noticed Kane on the sofa, and smiled weakly.

"I'm sorry about last night, Kane," Selena said timidly and with sincerity. "It's been a really bad week."

"Yeah, I'm sorry about last night too."

Despite his jealousy over a woman who technically wasn't even his yet, Kane decided to seize his moment alone with her. He was about to speak when she quickly changed the subject.

"Did Hayes show up yet?"

Refocusing on Hayes was for the best. "No, not yet," Kane informed her.

"What the hell--?" Selena bellowed.

There were more footfalls on the stairs followed by Riley and Casper's voices. Riley and Casper entered the lounge a moment later and appeared to be enjoying each other's company. Riley touched his arm while she laughed. Casper seemed to enjoy the way she touched him a little too much. Both looked at them as they entered the lounge.

"No Hayes," Selena informed Riley.

Riley's mood immediately turned cold. "Yeah, he called me a few minutes ago. He won't be here until later," she announced with the disgust evident in her voice.

"Yes!" Selena said excitedly.

Kane was almost as relieved as Selena. Hayes would miss the rockslide! He didn't know how it was possible, but Hayes had changed his own destiny. Kane just didn't understand why he remained trapped in the past.

"I'm going out to the site this morning as planned," Riley informed her.

"No!" Selena said with a frown.

Kane felt a shockwave go through his body. That was possibly the common denominator. Riley would go without Hayes, encounter the same rockslide, and somehow blame Selena. Perhaps Riley's injuries were what triggered her hostility toward Selena in the future. Maybe it was never about Hayes. He didn't know how, but he had to stop Riley from going.

"Someone has to be responsible and take charge around here," Riley informed her with the hostility evident in her tone. "I don't need Hayes' permission to do my job."

"No," Selena whined. "The others aren't up yet. That means you'll want me to go along."

That was even worse! If Riley took Selena, that might cause an entirely different set of ripples, which apparently brought them to the same outcome.

"You don't need to go, Selena," Riley replied.

"Yes--again!"

"You're not going alone," Kane firmly announced, now having enough of the emotional roller coaster he'd been riding.

All eyes were suddenly on Kane, including Casper's. Kane realized how that must have sounded and immediately fidgeted from the stares he received.

"Are you volunteering your chaperone services?" Riley teased and grinned in response.

Kane and Casper exchanged looks. Casper appeared horrified and shook his head in a secret signal.

"I'm not sure--" Kane began and searched for a response. "Maybe you should just wait until later." Later after the rockslide happens.

"No take backs," Riley announced cheerfully. "Go change into your hiking boots, city boy. You're in for two hours of hiking fun. I'll get the backpack and the map." Riley looked at Selena, who appeared clueless as to what just happened. "Will you get the emergency radio?"

"Yeah, sure. You've got it."

Selena and Riley left the lounge before either man could protest. Casper sat across from Kane on the sofa and stared at him with a look that chilled him.

"Dude, are you out of your mind?" Casper demanded softly. "That rockslide still happens, but this time it could be you killed in Hayes' place."

Kane appeared deep in thought and frantically searched for an answer. "I know, I'm thinking," he replied then looked at Casper. "What if when we reach that spot, I tell her it's too dangerous to cross?"

"How do you know that wasn't exactly what Hayes said?" Casper demanded.

"There's another trail."

"And it's twice as long," Casper announced sternly. "She'll never go for that."

"I won't give her a choice," Kane remarked boldly.

"As if you could stop her from doing whatever the hell she pleases," Casper scoffed.

"I'll take care of it," Kane informed him firmly. "If Hayes shows up, you can't let him come after us. I don't care if you have to tackle him to the ground and tie him up. Got it?"

"Yeah, man. I got it."

Chapter Twenty-one

The large horse stable located toward the back of the property allowed guests to rent horses by the hour or for the day and take picnic lunches along the trail. For the less adventurous, there was a romantic carriage to whisk couples away to their favorite, secluded lunch spot. Several well cared for horses grazed in the pasture beyond elegant, split rail fencing. Kane stood outside the barn and talked to the teenage stable boy, who gave him instructions along with a map of the trails. Two horses saddled in western tack were tied to the hitching post only a few feet away from the barn. Riley uncertainly approached while carrying her backpack, saw Kane with the saddled horses, and appeared bewildered. She paused near Kane and again looked at the horses.

"Casper said you were out here," Riley remarked. "What's going on?"

Kane grinned cheerfully and indicated his map. "We're taking the scenic route. I've rented some horses for the day. I thought it'd be fun."

"It's expensive and it'll take twice as long," she remarked sternly and appeared to disapprove with a look. "You do realize we'd have to take the longer trail."

Her tone concerned him, but he wasn't going to let that interfere with his plan. "Oh, I realize that," he muttered then grinned cheerfully. He was actually counting on that. "I've already paid to rent the horses. It's my treat."

"That's not really the point," Riley remarked.

Kane looked at her with a smile that mocked her. "Where's your sense of adventure?"

She stared at him a moment in silence then raised a brow while hiding her smile. "We're going to be in the saddle almost four hours one way, you know that?"

"Yippee ki yay," Kane said with a grin.

She appeared surprised then laughed and shook her head. "If this is what you really want to do, I'm game. Just remember, when you can't walk tomorrow, I was the voice of reason."

"I look forward to your teasing."

"You're going to regret those words, I promise," she informed him while holding back her laugh.

"Hmm, a challenge," he announced cheerfully. "I accept."

Riley shook her head and transferred the contents of her backpack into the saddlebag behind the saddle. She took the horse from the stable boy and swiftly mounted without hesitation or instruction. Kane took his horse and looked at Casper on the back patio in the near distance. Casper grinned and gave him two thumbs up. Kane mounted with little trouble and rode at a leisurely walk alongside Riley down the dirt driveway.

†

Casper piled bacon and eggs onto his plate from the overflowing buffet table within the empty dining room. There were many items including French toast, muffins, fresh fruit, home fries, and sausage in addition to the mounds of eggs and bacon. It would appear Casper had the entire breakfast buffet to himself that morning, and he wasn't about to let anything go to waste. His peaceful breakfast alone was interrupted when Collin and Chrissie entered. They looked around the mostly empty dining room then approached Casper by the buffet table. They each took a plate and checked over the morning offerings, which included hot beverages and a variety of fruit juices.

"What time did Hayes get here?" Collin asked Casper as he poured a cup of coffee.

Casper attempted to balance his loaded plate and didn't bother looking at Collin. It would be a tragedy if he lost any of his food to the floor.

"He called and said he wouldn't be here until this afternoon," Casper replied casually.

Collin and Chrissie exchanged looks and appeared equally surprised by the news.

"By the time he gets here, there won't be enough time to reach the expedition site and return before dark," Collin announced as irritation set in. "They'll either have to sleep outside tonight at the site or wait until tomorrow morning to go. It's going to put us a day behind."

"It's taken care of. Kane went with Riley to the site," Casper offered and attempted to balance his filled plate of food as he headed for the long table.

As he sat down, Collin joined him with his coffee and no food on his plate. He sat at the end of the table and stared at Casper, who didn't bother looking at him.

"Your friend went with Riley instead?" Collin suddenly demanded.

Casper cast a strange look at Collin. "Yeah, she insisted she was still going this morning, and Kane didn't think she should go alone, so he went with her," he remarked but wasn't about to let the odd comment go unquestioned. "I don't understand. Is there a problem with that?"

"Well, no," Collin remarked and suddenly appeared tense. "But it probably should have been me going. I wonder why Riley didn't just come and get me."

"Maybe she wanted to go with Kane."

"He's not a museum employee," Collin remarked.

"So? Maybe she thinks he's cute. He can be quite charming," Casper said while digging into his scrambled eggs. "I'm sure she knows what she's doing."

"She's strong-willed and pigheaded," Collin scoffed while leaning back in his chair with disgust.

"Maybe she took him along just to make Hayes jealous," Chrissie chimed in as she sat alongside Collin at the table with her plate of fruit.

"You haven't met Frank, the crazy bastard who owns rights to the find," Collin announced with an irritated sigh. "I don't think taking Kane along was such a good idea. Frank is completely paranoid."

"I'm sure Riley can handle him," Chrissie remarked and appeared less interested in the whole subject.

Collin didn't appear convinced but seemed willing to let it go. Casper played with his food a moment, although he didn't look up from his plate. It was obvious there was now something more on his mind.

Chapter Twenty-two

Kane and Riley rode their horses alongside each other on the wide, well-groomed path at a leisurely walk. The forest was peaceful and secluded in the morning hour. It almost seemed as if they were the only two people alive. Kane actually found the ride hypnotic and relaxing. It was possibly the first time he'd felt relaxed since Selena had been killed. Even though he was sharing the lengthy morning with Riley, the woman he'd assume kill then look at, he couldn't help feeling content. He found it odd that she hadn't spoken throughout most of the ride. He wasn't sure if that was a good or bad thing. Obviously, it was good for him. He didn't really want to talk to her anyway. He preferred the solitude while riding in such peaceful surroundings. Mindless chatter from the woman who later kills his girlfriend was the last thing he needed. Still--? Her silence somehow bothered him. He resisted looking at her. She glanced at him several times and smiled almost playfully.

"Almost two hours in the saddle and not one complaint from you," Riley teased, finally breaking the silence.

Kane was almost relieved that she finally spoke. He wasn't even sure why. He smiled and shrugged. "I did a lot of riding when I was a boy. I always wanted to be a cowboy. Then I turned twelve and discovered girls--"

"Should have found yourself a nice little cowgirl," she teased and seductively raised her brows.

"At twelve, I wasn't that smart."

Riley laughed softly and studied the scenery, again falling silent. Kane finally felt compelled to look at her. He studied her a long moment in silence and became curious about her for the first time. He wasn't sure why it mattered, but he wanted to know more about her.

"What *is* between you and Hayes?" Kane finally asked. He couldn't believe he asked that question and immediately cursed himself for saying it aloud.

She glanced at him and appeared almost surprised by the forwardness of his question then resumed looking at the scenery and smiled. "I was fifteen when I first started working with Hayes at the museum," she informed him with a grin. "He's my best friend, and I love him very much." There was an odd silence. "But there's nothing between us."

Kane studied her and appeared deep in thought.

She caught his look and suddenly chuckled. "You have that look of doubt."

"No, I believe you," Kane replied, feeling slightly embarrassed, and couldn't help but smile. "How did you come to work for Hayes at such a young age?"

"I've always been fascinated with the museum," she casually replied. "I practically lived there during the summer while growing up, so they let me help out. I kind of knew my way around more than most, so when Hayes was hired as curator, they put me on as his helper." She appeared humored and grinned slyly at Kane. "He absolutely hated me. Of course, when Hayes first showed up, he hated everyone. He was a miserable prick most of his life. His parents were very rich and twice as unfeeling. It took me the entire summer to turn him into a caring human being."

Kane was amused by her candor. "Killed him with kindness, huh?"

Her eyes suddenly widened. "Oh, no, the opposite," she announced while laughing. "I fought fire with fire. It was a battle of the wills, and mine was stronger."

"Sounds risky. You could have been fired," Kane remarked but couldn't help feeling intrigued by her boldness. "You're lucky it worked out."

"At fifteen, I had very little to lose," she announced with a shrug. "It actually wasn't that difficult. Despite our feuds behind closed doors, I did everything in my power to build him up to those who mattered, including giving him credit for my ideas. I made him look good. Eventually he turned into the man I built up in everyone's mind."

Kane desperately wanted to know the connection. Hayes death obviously had fueled her revenge. It just didn't seem possible that she wasn't in love with him. He just couldn't understand what happened.

"You seem very protective of him," Kane finally remarked. "I suppose that's why some would assume there's more to your relationship."

"Believe me, almost everyone at the museum has assumed there's more to our relationship, but none of the rumors are true," she informed him. "I suppose I could fight the battle and insist profoundly that there's nothing between us, but I allow them to think what they want to maintain Hayes' image. He denies there's anything between us to others, but I know it makes him feel good that they think there is." She grinned at Kane and casually shrugged. "His ego can use the stroking."

"I'm surprised you'd do that for him," Kane replied. "I mean, sacrifice your reputation to build Hayes' ego."

"Ours is a complex relationship," she informed him. "Make no mistake, Hayes would die for me; and I'd almost certainly kill for him."

Kane stared at her with a sobering realization to her comment. She had so little in common with her evil counterpart from the future, but there was no mistaken this was the same woman. Scarred Riley was lurking just beyond her eyes, and he couldn't deny the thought chilled him.

†

*T*he wine cellar was a stunning work of art. The massive, stone room was filled with racks containing hundreds of bottles of wine. The wine varied in type and vintage. There were two, heavy wooden tables with chairs in the center of the room. Bessie removed one of the slightly dusty bottles and showed it to Casper while grinning proudly. Casper eyed the bottle then looked at her with surprise.

"That's some old wine," he announced.

She carefully replaced the bottle to its rightful place in the rack. "I've been collecting vintage wine for over twenty years," she remarked. "My family used to own a vineyard. Sadly, it was taken from them a long time ago. I guess this is my way of holding on to that ideal."

"Have any of your family's label?"

Bessie grinned with delight to his interest and quickly darted down the aisle. She removed another bottle and showed it to him. Casper glanced at the bottle and nodded his approval.

"Think you'll ever drink it?"

She frowned and shrugged. "I doubt it. I was saving it for my twenty-fifth wedding anniversary. We never even made it to our tenth."

"I'm sorry to hear," Casper said gently.

"I'm not," she replied a little too quickly. "He never wanted any part of the whole country inn thing. Once he was out of the picture, I was finally able to fulfill some of my dreams."

"Then you should celebrate on your twenty-fifth anniversary of being an innkeeper," Casper suggested.

"Somehow I don't think I'll feel like celebrating," she remarked with a depressed sigh. "I enjoy the company, but it's an empty existence."

"You know what you should do," he announced boldly. "Have singles weekends or maybe wine tasting events. Attract guests with which you have something in common. You're totally missing the boat. You can create your own fulfillment."

Bessie appeared to consider his suggestion. "You know, you may be right."

"I know I'm right," he informed her while grinning proudly. "I have a sharp mind. The world doesn't know how lucky it is that I use it for good and not evil."

She laughed softly and affectionately touched his arm. The phone was heard ringing from upstairs, alerting her. "I'd better get that," she announced and hurried up the stairs.

Casper watched her run up the steps, tilted his head, and appeared to entertain a wayward thought or two. He quickly dismissed his inappropriate thoughts, walked along the aisles, and looked around casually. A few minutes passed when someone was heard on the stone steps. He walked out of the aisle expecting to see Bessie. Selena walked along the wine rack and removed one of the bottles without even looking at it. She took the bottle and headed for the stairs. Casper appeared surprised and hurried after her.

"Hey, wait," he announced.

Selena stopped and appeared surprised to see him in the wine cellar. Her look revealed her loath for him. "What do you want?" she asked curtly.

"You can't take a bottle of wine without permission," he informed her. "That would be rude."

"Yeah, whatever," she snapped. "I'll pay for it."

"You don't understand," he remarked more sternly. "Bessie collects wine. That may be part of her collection and not for consumption."

"What's with you?" Selena demanded with look of disgust in her eyes.

"What's with me? What's with you?" Casper remarked boldly and glared at her snobby expression. "You certainly don't care much about anyone other than yourself."

"I certainly don't care about you or what you think, if that's what you mean," she retorted and continued toward the steps with the bottle of wine.

Casper darted in front of her and cut off her path to the stairs. His agility considering his size almost certainly surprised her, and she wasn't getting past his large frame that now filled the doorway. "You're not taking that bottle with you--not without Bessie's permission."

"Why? Are you going to tell on me?" she asked as her upper lip curved into a sneer.

"Yes, I will."

"Fine," she scoffed and shoved the bottle into his chest.

Casper attempted to catch the bottle. It fell from his hands and shattered on the stone floor. Both stared at the shattered bottle and spilled wine.

Selena was only momentarily surprised then snorted a laugh. "I guess you're in trouble." She casually walked past him and up the stairs.

Casper stared at the broken bottle with his mouth hanging open then looked after Selena with surprise. He shook his head with disgust and immediately turned hostile. "There's no way I'm being best man at that wedding."

As Casper searched the wine cellar for a dustpan, he heard a loud, female gasp.

"Oh, my God!"

He hurried toward the stairs and saw Bessie staring at the broken bottle. Casper immediately fidgeted and obviously felt terrible.

"I'm so sorry, Bessie," he quickly attempted to explain. "It was an accident--"

Bessie took a deep breath then offered a tiny smile and waved her hand. "It's okay, Casper," she announced and seemingly produced a dustpan and brush from nowhere. "It happens. It wasn't worth very much."

Casper stared at her a moment then smiled while shaking his head. "You are one classy lady."

Chapter Twenty-three

*K*ane and Riley arrived in a clearing near the exploration site and stopped their horses alongside a large tree. Both dismounted and tied the horses to the tree while looking around. Everything appeared quiet. For some reason, it bothered Kane. There was a dusty four-wheeler parked near a tent by the stream. The cave was fifty yards away with an entrance that was barely visible if one wasn't looking for it. It seemed as if their friend, Frank, had purposely moved brush and branches closer to the cave entrance to conceal it. Kane remembered the unflattering things Hayes had said about the man they were about to meet. They approached the cave entrance.

"Wait until you meet this guy," Riley announced with a look of humor. "He's one of those survivalist types jacked up on caffeine. Don't be surprised if he greets us with a shotgun." Riley stopped him just outside the cave entrance. "Frank, it's Riley!" There was no response. "Frank!'

There was still no response. Riley shrugged and entered the cave.

"Is that a good idea?" Kane asked as he uncertainly followed her through the opening.

The cramped cave was dimly lit by strategically placed lanterns lining the walls. The cave itself had been around since the eighteen hundreds. Most of the support beams were rotted and leaned on frightening angles. Kane wasn't getting good vibes from this particular expedition, although Riley hadn't a care in the world. A lantern further down was extinguished, leaving a large, dark area nearly fifty feet ahead. Riley removed a small flashlight as Kane followed her.

"Maybe we should wait for an invitation," Kane remarked.

"We were invited, remember?" She then appeared to consider and grinned. "Well, I was. He might shoot you on principle," she teased.

He glared at her. "Not funny."

Riley hid her smile but remained amused by his concern. "Are you scared of the dark, Kane?"

"No, the man with the shotgun is enough."

Riley paused within the cave, turned toward him, and suddenly moved uncomfortably close while grinning deviously. "Maybe it's me you're afraid of."

There was a distinct possibility that was the case. He wasn't sure he liked her being so close to him, especially in such close, dark quarters. He certainly couldn't let her think it had anything to do with her.

"Don't be ridiculous."

Kane wished he sounded more confident. A rabbit darted past them and into the cave, startling him. Kane jumped and looked around. Riley took another step closer to him and maintained her playful tone.

"It was just a rabbit," she teased while grinning. "You're jumpy."

Kane uncertainly moved away from her. He couldn't stop thinking about the last time she was that close to him and the pain she caused when she kicked him in the face. Riley appeared surprised by his retreat and laughed.

"Oh, my God, you are afraid of me! What did I ever do to you?" she teased.

"That's a loaded question," Kane muttered.

She moved closer to him, touched his chest, and appeared particularly playful. "I've never frightened a man before," she cooed almost seductively. "It's kind of fun."

Kane again moved away from her and closer to the entrance while attempting to sound more confident. He shamefully felt the need to duck out the entrance. "You don't scare me--"

"Then why do you keep moving away?"

Kane realized she was right, and he resisted the urge to move away from her. After all, what was she really going to do? She certainly wasn't going to attack him as she had that night in the museum. Riley moved against him, placed her hands to his shoulders, and kissed him warmly on the lips. Kane suddenly tensed with surprise and possible horror to her soft lips on his. He actually hadn't seen that coming. Her lustful actions were troubling and puzzling. His heart was pounding, which seemed only natural, but he wished other parts of his body stopped reacting with so much enthusiasm. He cursed his genitals for being easily manipulated. Riley pulled back, met his stunned gazed, and appeared disappointed despite her smirk.

"Not nearly as good as I had imagined," she remarked with disappointment in her tone.

A thousand thoughts raced through Kane's mind as he stared at her. He didn't know if he wanted to kill her or kiss her, but he was almost positive he wanted to punch himself in the groin to teach his genitals a lesson. The rabbit running through the cave suddenly caught his attention and took his focus off his own arousal. As the rabbit ran into the darkened area, Kane noticed a thin wire across the cave floor just inches from the ground. He attempted to make sense of the wire, anything to take his mind off Riley's kiss, when the rabbit ran into the wire. There was a loud explosion as the cave rumbled. For a moment, he was paralyzed with shock. Riley threw him out the entrance as the cave collapsed behind them. Riley and Kane roughly hit the ground outside the cave. Dirt, dust, and rocks erupted from the entrance in a large, dark cloud. Riley attempted to look back at the destruction. Kane dove on top of her and shielded her with his body as debris flew past them. They were pelted with small rocks and rotting wood fragments. The debris finally settled. Kane slowly rolled off Riley and looked at the sealed entrance just a few feet behind them. Riley slowly sat up and appeared horrified.

"Frank--" Riley gasped.

"I saw a tripwire," Kane cried out while jumping to his feet with added soreness. He immediately regretted the sudden action. "That idiot had the cave rigged to explode!"

"He's crazy, but he's not that crazy," she cried out as she remained sitting on the ground and stared at the sealed cave just before them.

Kane looked back at Riley, took her hand, and helped her to her feet. Both brushed thick amounts of dirt from them. Kane looked at the abrasions and cuts on her arms through the thick layer of dirt covering her then noticed the small cut on her cheek. He placed his hand to her chin and assessed her injury. It was in the exact spot where she later had the scar, although this injury was only minor. Kane stared longer than he should. It was an eerie reminder of who she later became. He had to force himself to say something to get that image out of his head.

"Are you okay?" Kane uncertainly asked.

Riley slowly nodded and gingerly rubbed her sore wrist. "That was one hell of a tackle," she announced. "Remind me to never piss you off."

He suddenly tensed and allowed his thoughts to drift momentarily. "I'll be sure to do that," Kane muttered.

Riley hurried for the startled, tied horses now covered in dirt and removed her emergency two-way radio from the saddlebag. "Selena, do you copy?"

There was no sound. Riley attempted a different frequency. There was still no sound. She popped the back casing off the radio. The batteries were missing! Her expression turned to rage, frightening Kane.

"Damn it, Selena! She gives dumb blondes a bad name!" Riley cried out.

Kane appeared bewildered and stared at the radio. Was that the incident that ultimately led to Selena's murder? Did she blame Selena because she couldn't call for help when Hayes died? Riley shook her head in disgust.

"Frank could be buried alive in that cave. You stay here," she ordered. "I'm going to take the four-wheeler for help."

Kane's mind raced with a flood of concern and fright. "I don't think you should go alone."

"I'm fine. Selena's the one you need to worry about!" she lashed out.

Kane stared at her with surprise. Her anger and hatred was frightening, but this time no one died. Selena should be spared, but if that was the case, why hadn't he vanished as Casper had predicted. Could Casper have been wrong about the entire time displacement theory? A tall, lanky man held his head as he stumbled toward them from beyond the tent. Riley saw Frank, appeared relieved, and ran for him.

"Frank, thank God!"

Frank stared at the cave-in with a look of horror then glared at her. "What the hell did you do?"

"Me?" Riley suddenly slapped his arm. Frank jumped and bolted away from her. "What's wrong with you? You nearly killed us with that booby trap!"

"What? No. Are you insane? Why would I blow up the mine?" he demanded while gesturing wildly. "There's a fortune in there. Now look at it! It'll take months to dig that out!"

"There was a tripwire," Kane announced firmly.

"Tripwire?" Frank suddenly demanded while giving Kane a distrusting once over. "I didn't rig the mine to explode. How stupid are you?"

Riley and Kane rolled their eyes. Kane had to resist the urge to punch the man. He wasn't much of a fighter, but this situation almost definitely called for it. Riley then noticed Frank's bleeding head.

"What happened to you?" Riley asked.

Frank waved her off. "Ah, a damned rock must've hit me on the head. Knocked me out cold," he informed her. "This whole area is unstable. Rocks falling everywhere."

"I'd say this expedition is officially over," Kane firmly insisted. He'd had enough for one day. "It's a long ride back. We should get going."

Chapter Twenty-four

*T*he bed and breakfast lobby was peaceful that afternoon. The entire inn seemed unusually quiet. There hadn't been a soul around since breakfast, which seemed strange considering how many guests were staying within the old inn. Casper sat on one of the lounge chairs with a mug of hot chocolate setting on the coffee table alongside the coaster that clearing indicated it should be used. He relaxed with a large, homemade cookie in one hand and a gossip magazine in the other while his large feet were proudly propped on the coffee table. Judging by the amount of cookie crumbs surrounding him and spread across his shirt, he'd had a few cookies already. A loud thump was heard from upstairs. Casper looked to the ceiling and appeared bewildered. When he didn't hear any other sounds, he returned to his magazine. The front door was heard opening. Casper glanced up as Hayes entered. Casper sprang to his feet, allowing cookie crumbs to scatter along the floor.

"Hey, there you are!" Casper announced cheerfully. "Did you get lost?"

Hayes approached the check in desk and set his overnight bag down with a low sigh. "No, I needed to take care of a few personal things before I came out here." He seemed to tense slightly. "Is Riley upset?"

"Maybe she was a little," Casper replied and flicked a crumb from his shirt while missing the other six. "I assume she got over it. She was in a good mood when she and Kane headed out to the site this morning."

Hayes appeared surprised and stared at Casper a long moment. "She went without me?"

"Yeah, she was insistent about going, so Kane went with her," he replied.

"She shouldn't have done that," Hayes remarked and seemed intensely concerned. "Did they take a radio? I should probably check on them and make sure everything is okay."

"Of course everything's okay," Casper informed him. "They took a map and everything. Kane won't let anything happen to her. Stop worrying."

"I don't know," he announced and fidgeted. "Maybe I should go out there. If anything happens, I'll feel responsible."

Casper's entire body suddenly twitched to his comment about going to the expedition site. "Nothing's going to happen," Casper said almost too quickly then fumbled to sound more relaxed. "Kane's an excellent rider, and Riley seemed at home in the saddle."

Hayes appeared surprised. "They rode out on horseback?"

"Yeah," Casper informed him. "Kane was all, like, 'oh, horses'. He's weird."

"If they took horses, they had to take the longer trail," Hayes remarked. He appeared to consider the thought then smiled and laughed softly. "That's a long time in the saddle."

"Yeah, Kane's gonna be hurting," Casper announced while grinning.

The door opened to reveal Collin. He saw Hayes, hesitated a moment, and then appeared unusually cheerful. "I see you finally made it."

"Yes," Hayes replied dryly. "Apparently Riley didn't bother to wait for me either."

"Well, you know Riley," Collin teased. "Once she gets something into her head--" He collapsed onto one of the nearby chairs and appeared curious. "I was just out for a walk, and I saw a strange car parked in the woods."

"A strange car?" Hayes asked then brushed it off. "Maybe it broke down." He then appeared to reconsider. "What makes it strange?"

"It sort of looked like Randy's car," Collin remarked.

"You mean the Randy I fired last week?" Hayes asked with surprise.

"That's why I thought it seemed strange. Think he's secretly seeing Chrissie?" Collin asked with a note of jealousy in his tone. "I hope she didn't invite him."

"Chrissie's here," Hayes asked with a puzzled look.

"Yeah," Collin replied. "I thought we could use the extra hands."

Casper stared at both men then felt the need to interrupt by waving his hands around. "Whoa, whoa, back it up a minute," he suddenly announced. "A man gets fired then shows up at a remote inn where his boss is working." Casper appeared concerned. "Isn't anyone else a little troubled by that? Sounds more like a plot for revenge to me."

Hayes and Collin suddenly looked at Casper. Collin appeared concerned and looked back at Hayes.

"I heard he was lurking around the museum a few days after he was fired," Collin suddenly remarked.

Hayes groaned and shook his head. "He wasn't lurking, he was cleaning out his locker. I sincerely doubt Randy came all the way out here to the sticks to beat me senseless."

Casper uncertainly sat while staring at Hayes. It was obvious his mind was reeling with the new information. The sound of thundering footfalls were heard on the stairs, alerting all three men. Tucker appeared at the bottom of the stairs with his overnight bag, stormed across the lobby past them, and out the door. Selena hurried after him. All three men exchanged bewildered looks.

"What the hell is he doing here?" Hayes suddenly asked.

Casper jumped up from his chair and hurried to the window closest to the porch. Selena and Tucker's voices were heard shouting. Casper glanced at Hayes and Collin, who stared at him with apparent disapproval.

Casper frowned. "I suppose it's rude to eavesdrop."

"Keep it down," Collin shushed him. "I can't hear."

Casper hid his smile and returned to listening by the window.

Tucker stormed off the porch and approached his car in the lot alongside the other parked cars. Selena was on his heels. He tossed his bag into the backseat and slammed the door. Selena stood before the driver's side door, folded her arms across her chest, and glared at him.

"I wasn't finished talking to you," she growled.

"You weren't talking; you were screaming like a banshee," he snapped.

"Where the hell do you think you're going?"

"Anywhere you're not," he announced while glaring at her. "Since I've met you, you've been nothing but trouble. You're a spoiled little girl trapped in a woman's body. When things don't go your way, you stomp your foot and throw a tantrum. I'm tired of being some pawn in your sick, little game. I'm not letting you take me down with you."

"Oh, you're the pawn? I'm using you, huh?" she demanded while glaring at him. "That's hysterical!"

"Hey, I don't need this crap!" he launched back. "Now get out of my way!"

"Fine," she screamed and moved away from the car door. "But don't come crawling back to me! It's over!"

Tucker opened the driver's side door and glared at her. "No kidding it's over! I'm the one ending it!" He sneered at her. "Have a nice life, bitch."

Tucker jumped into the car, started it, and burned out in reverse. Selena appeared to pout while watching him speed down the gravel driveway. She stomped her foot then appeared to consider the action. She frowned and hurried for the porch. As Selena entered the inn, Casper and Collin leaped onto nearby chairs and attempted to act disinterested. Hayes remained standing near the front desk as Selena slammed the door. She suddenly hesitated and looked at the three men in the room. She seemed to calm slightly.

"I suppose you heard that," she remarked with some hostility.

"Heard what?" Collin asked with an innocent look on his face then quickly turned his magazine facing the right direction.

"I never understood that relationship anyway," Hayes remarked simply, causing both men to stare at him.

"So you *were* listening," Selena pouted.

"Selena, they heard you out on the interstate," Hayes informed her while casually placing his hands in his pockets. "Riley warned you about Tucker."

Selena groaned and ran up the stairs. Collin and Casper eyed Hayes with marvel and shook their heads.

"Did you purposely engage her?" Collin asked. "Why would you do that?"

Hayes shrugged. "I'm a prick."

"Some of my closest friends are pricks," Casper casually announced.

"You never liked Selena," Collin remarked.

"She makes bad personal choices," he replied. "She's on the short trip to self-destruct and won't listen to anyone who tries to help her.   The only thing left to do is sit back and watch her explode."

"I feel sorry for the idiot who marries her," Casper muttered and finished his cookie.

"I don't know," Collin announced.   "Maybe now with Tucker out of her life, she'll finally grow up.   He doesn't exactly bring out the best in women."

Albert entered the lobby and looked around.   "What's all that shouting and banging?" he asked.   "I thought this was supposed to be a relaxing rat trap."

"Excuse me," came Bessie's harsh voice from nearby.

All four looked at Bessie approaching from the hallway.   She glared at Albert through piercing eyes.

"Did you just call my inn a rat trap?" she demanded to know while placing her hands on her hips.   Judging by the color in her face, Bessie was the one who was about to explode.

"I'm sure you misunderstood him," Collin quickly announced while standing.

"No, I'm pretty sure he said 'rat trap'," Hayes commented with little emotion.

Albert glared at Hayes.

Bessie suddenly poked Albert in the chest while glaring at him. "I have put my blood and sweat into this place," Bessie proclaimed while throwing around her hands.   "Who the hell do you think you are calling my inn a rat trap!"

Casper and Collin sheepishly hurried across the lobby and out the front door.   Hayes smirked and leaned against the check in desk while watching Albert back away from the irate woman and fumble for an apology.

Chapter Twenty-five

$\mathcal{I}$t was late afternoon and a warm breeze blew past the back porch where Hayes sat on one of the rocking chairs with a glass of iced tea on the table alongside him. He stared into the vast countryside of fields and woods while appearing lost in his own thoughts. Selena walked onto the porch, saw him sitting in the rocking chair, and uncertainly leaned against the railing across from him. She avoided looking at him and had the appearance of a scolded child attempting to get out of being grounded.

"I'm sorry about my behavior earlier," she said softly. "You were right about Tucker, of course."

He looked at her and smiled timidly. "I probably could have been a little more sensitive while pointing that out," Hayes informed her. "You know he's bad for you."

"Yeah, I know."

"So now it's time to start making good decisions," he announced.

She slowly nodded and finally looked at him. She smiled timidly. "You know, not all of us are like Riley. We don't all have someone like you looking out for us." Her head again lowered and she spoke softly. "I wish I had someone like you looking out for me."

Hayes studied her a moment in silence and was about to speak when he looked past her. His expression suddenly dropped and he appeared alarmed by what he saw. He slowly stood and stared at the distant woods.

"What the hell--?"

Selena looked in the direction he stared. Kane and Riley could be seen riding along the edge of the woods. Both horse and riders were covered in a thick layer of dirt. Hayes bolted from the porch. Selena hurried after him. Riley and Kane rode their horses along the woods' edge toward the stables behind the inn. Frank followed behind them on his four-wheeler. All three were exhausted and covered with dirt and scratches. Selena and Hayes hurried toward them from the back porch. Kane and Riley slowly dismounted with added stiffness as the stable boy collected their horses. The poor kid was speechless over the filthy condition in which they were returning the horses. Hayes approached Riley, pulled her into his arms, and looked over her with concern.

"Riley, what happened? Are you okay?" Hayes asked and didn't seem to care that their closeness was getting his expensive clothes dirty.

She allowed him to fuss over her minor scrapes and bruises, but she obviously didn't care for all the attention. "There was a cave-in at the mine," she replied with disgust.

Frank appeared annoyed and approached them. "And for the last time, I didn't do it," he snapped.

"Thank God you're okay," Selena gasped.

Riley pulled away from Hayes and spun toward Selena with rage in her eyes. "No thanks to you!"

"What?"

"There weren't any batteries in the damned radio!" Riley shouted. "If any of us had been badly injured, we'd be in serious trouble!"

"Of course there were batteries! I swear I checked!" Selena protested.

"Ah, save it!"

Riley stormed away from the stables and headed for the inn. Hayes appeared surprised by Riley's outburst then hurried after her. Selena watched them head for the inn, appeared upset, and lowered her head. Kane uncertainly approached Selena and attempted to smooth things over.

"It wasn't your fault," Kane said gently. "She's just upset. It's been a rough day."

"Thanks. Tell her that, okay?" Selena touched his arm, offered a tiny smile, and then headed for the inn.

Casper approached Kane and stared at his battered and bruised body with surprise. "Dude, you're a mess."

"Thanks for noticing," Kane muttered. He sighed and shut his eyes. It had been one hell of a day. "Disaster was averted. Tell me it's over."

"I hate to bring you down, but if disaster was actually averted, you wouldn't be here. If Selena doesn't die, you wouldn't time travel," Casper informed him. "I don't know why you're still here, but it's not over."

Kane was horrified by Casper's comment. "But Hayes didn't die," he protested as panic swept through him. "Sure, Riley's mad at Selena, but she's not going to kill her over a few bumps and bruises. She'll get over that."

"I'll rack my brains over it," Casper replied. "I'll come up with something." He then grinned deviously. "Hey, you missed it. Tucker and Selena got into one hell of a fight an hour or so ago. He packed his bag and tore out of here. Great news, huh?"

"Maybe if I didn't feel like I'd been run over by a truck, I'd feel like celebrating."

†

*H*ayes sat facing a freshly showered Riley at the kitchen table while applying ointment to the cut on her cheek near her eye. Despite his gentleness, she cringed and jerked slightly. He hesitated and gave her a stern, disapproving look. She appeared scolded and hid her embarrassed smile.

"Another centimeter and you could have lost your eye," he informed her.

"Another foot into the cave, and I'd have lost a lot more than an eye," she informed him.

Hayes made a face to her comment. The reality of it hit a little close to home. "You shouldn't have gone out there without me. What were you thinking?"

"That my boss should have showed up when he was supposed to," she remarked.

He glared at her about to protest then immediately frowned. "You're right, of course. I should have been here," Hayes muttered softly. "I should have assumed you'd be stubborn enough to go out on your own."

"I wasn't alone," she bluntly informed him. "I went with Kane."

"Who barely brought you back in one piece," Hayes scoffed while sneering.

"This wasn't Kane's fault," she informed him.

"No, you're right. It wasn't," Hayes replied but remained hostile. "It's Frank's fault, and I'll be sure to have words with him about it."

"Kane said enough words for the both of you," she replied. "Let it go."

Hayes was about to protest when he caught her stern glare. It was one argument he wasn't going to win. Hayes frowned and returned to her injury. He dried the cut then delicately placed tiny adhesive strips over it to hold it together. Kane, who was now showered and changed, appeared on the back stairs while holding a cloth to his bleeding arm. The bleeding had stopped, but the hot shower dissolved the dirt-caked scab and reopened it. He saw the two in the kitchen and stopped to watch Hayes affectionately tending to Riley's cut near her eye. Hayes' feelings for his young assistant were evident by the way he cared for her injuries. It was almost intimate, leaving Kane feeling as if he was interrupting a moment between the two. He looked down while deep in thought, frowned, and headed back up the stairs before either saw him.

Chapter Twenty-six

Casper entered the dining room and approached the beverage station. The cookie plate contained only crumbs. He frowned and lifted the plate, making certain none had found their way beneath the plate. He set the empty plate down with disgust. He smelled the air and looked toward the open kitchen door. A devious smile crossed his face. Casper quietly entered the kitchen. The large, rustic kitchen was empty, and Bessie was nowhere to be found. More than a dozen large chocolate chip cookies were lined along the counter to cool. Casper grinned and approached the freshly baked cookies. He picked one up and bit into it. It was warm and gooey. Casper rolled his eyes and groaned with delight. Soft angry voices were heard from the dining room, catching his attention. He moved closer to the open door to listen.

"If you had followed through with your original plan," Collin announced, "we wouldn't have this problem."

"I used every connection I had," Albert remarked lowly. "It's not my fault Hayes has god status at the museum. I want him fired as badly as you, but there was nothing I could do."

"So is that why you went to plan B?"

"What are you talking about?" Albert suddenly demanded to know.

"Don't play stupid, Mercer," Collin scoffed with irritation in his voice. "Frank's crazy, but he's not crazy enough to rig his own mine to blow."

"You think I--?"

"No, I think you had your 'associate' do it for you," Collin announced softly. "No one saw him since last night. He could have easily slipped out there and did the deed."

"You're insane," Albert lashed out softly. "He didn't slip out to the mine. He's attending to other matters for me. He'll be back in the morning. Besides, Grier took the car. Do you think he drove to the mine? Correct me if I'm wrong, but only the three of you know where the mine is even located."

"All I know is, I don't want to get involved in whatever it is you're plotting," Collin snapped. "Just leave me out of it. I won't be a party to killing people for some stupid promotion."

Their voices trailed off. Casper remained near the open doorway and sank into thought. It was obvious their conversation had him concerned. A woman cleared her throat from behind him. Casper glanced back and saw Bessie staring at him with her arms folded across her chest and her brow cleverly raised. She indicated the cookie in his hand.

"You could have asked."

Casper grinned sheepishly having been caught pilfering cookies. Bessie then laughed. He groaned softly as his shoulders sagged with relief.

✝

Later that afternoon. Kane entered the lounge while off in another world. He uncertainly stopped when he saw Riley sitting on one of the sofas with a drink in her hand. She appeared moderately distracted as well and didn't notice he had entered. Something between them suddenly felt oddly different. He wasn't sure what had him bothered, but he contemplated leaving before she noticed him. She looked up from her drink and saw him. Having been caught staring at her, he knew he couldn't just turn and leave, so he approached her. Riley grinned and appeared humored.

"You're not walking so good these days," Riley teasingly pointed out. "Is that saddle soreness, or did someone try to blow you up?"

He snorted a soft laugh at her warped sense of humor--even if it was at his expense. "A little of both, I'm afraid. How are you feeling?" Kane asked and sat on the sofa near her. He didn't know why he cared, but he did.

"Aside from feeling like I'd been tackled by a linebacker, I'm feeling pretty good," she replied then grinned slyly. "But that's probably the tequila."

Kane chuckled. Riley smiled and affectionately touched his lower arm. His expression dropped as he stared into her dark eyes. He was suddenly concerned that her touch no longer sent feelings of rage through him.

"I'm grateful for your timely tackle," Riley said softly with sincerity.

Something stirred inside him. He gently cleared his throat while feeling oddly insecure and embarrassed. "Hey, we wouldn't be here if it wasn't for those cat-like reflexes of yours," he announced with a tiny grin. The more he thought about, the more he realized she did in fact save his life with how quickly she reacted. Also, if she hadn't stopped him to flirt as she did, it could have cost them their lives instead of the poor rabbit. "That explosion stopped me in my tracks. I wasn't expecting the entire mine to come down around us. I can't believe you kept your wits like that."

Riley smiled and shrugged while sipping her drink. "I used to spend my summers with my crazy uncle. His idea of fun was paintball battles and karate training," she teased. "You learn to react quickly when you're the only girl in a paintball battle against six ex-Marines reliving the glory days."

"Karate, huh?" he asked while considering the way she tossed him around at the museum five years from now. "Are you any good?"

Riley grinned and raised her brows deviously. "Let's hope you never find out."

Kane smirked knowingly. He already found out the hard way. Riley stared into his eyes a moment then kissed him quickly but warmly on the lips. She pulled away while smiling, stood, and quickly left the lounge without further comment. Kane appeared stunned and watched her leave. Casper approached and watched her leave as well.

"You were looking at her ass, weren't you?" Casper suddenly asked, startling Kane with his sudden appearance.

Kane felt embarrassed by his friend's accusation. He wasn't staring at her ass. At least, he didn't think he was staring at her ass. "Don't be stupid."

"I obviously missed something," Casper remarked. "What happened?"

"Nothing," Kane muttered while fidgeting with discomfort. "Any thoughts about why I'm still here?"

"All I can come up with is that you couldn't have changed the future," Casper informed him. "For some unknown reason, Riley must still kill Selena."

"That's impossible," Kane protested with disgust. "The accident was prevented."

Casper appeared preoccupied while deep in thought then looked at Kane with concern. "Don't you find it ironic that the same day Hayes supposedly dies in a rockslide, you two are nearly killed in an exploding mineshaft?"

"That's because that idiot Frank set a booby trap," Kane scoffed with detest.

"What if he didn't?" Casper asked while raising his brows in question. "What if *neither* was an accident?"

Kane stared at Casper and was surprised or possibly horrified by the suggestion. "You think someone wanted to kill Hayes? But who? Why?" He was then lost in his own thoughts. "Riley would be so lost without him--"

"I knew it. You're hot for her!" Casper suddenly announced while grinning. "You dog!"

Kane was stunned by the accusation. "I'm in love with Selena, remember?"

"And she's in love with Tucker. There's no reason why you can't make a play for Riley. It's not cheating. Who'd know?"

"I would know," Kane remarked firmly. "That makes it's cheating."

"Are you kidding? Right now, the other you is dogging some girl at that city nightclub," Casper remarked while waving him off carelessly. "I'm beginning to think you're never going to make your move on that one."

He considered Casper's comment then grinned almost lustfully. "Oh, yeah. Connie." Kane reflected then frowned. "That doesn't pan out for another three months. Incidentally, three months from now, make sure I get some new condoms. You'll save me a lot of stress."

"You've got it," Casper replied then tilted his head and appeared curious. "So what do you intend to do about Riley?"

Kane groaned at his friend's persistent desire to hook him up with Riley. "I don't intend to do anything about her," Kane informed him. "I'm not hot for her. If you saw what she did to Selena, you'd understand."

"No offense, but I'd rather see you with Riley," Casper remarked. "I'm not exactly fond of Selena."

"You'll learn to like her," Kane replied but no longer felt convinced. "You two get along just fine in the future. I guess you just got off to a bad start--"

"A bad start?" Casper interjected. "She's a monster!"

Kane frowned his disapproval but didn't have any argument to convince Casper otherwise. At the moment, he almost felt like agreeing with him.

Chapter Twenty-seven

Collin entered the second floor hallway from his guestroom and nearly collided with Noble, who seemed overly excited about something. His eyes were wide and his grin nearly matched.

"Did you hear?" Noble asked.

"Hear what?" Collin replied with great curiosity.

"Riley and that Kane fellow were nearly killed by a cave-in," he announced while maintaining his grin.

Collin stared at Noble with a strange look on his face. "Yeah, I heard. And you're grinning because--?"

"Relax," Noble snapped then sneered. "They both survived. That whack job Frank nearly did them in. It's just kind of funny, that's all."

Collin rolled his eyes and walked toward the stairs. "There's something not right in your head, Noble."

He followed Collin down the stairs. "Do you have any idea how many times Riley has made me look bad? I think I'm entitled to enjoy a little of her misery. Just because you wouldn't mind getting in her pants--"

"I never said I wanted to get into her pants," Collin snapped and attempted to ignore him.

Noble just rolled his eyes as if knowing something Collin wasn't willing to share. The two walked in silence toward the lounge and fresh coffee. They entered the lounge and immediately noticed Chrissie sitting on Albert's lap while the two kissed aggressively and groped each other. Collin stopped and stared with a stunned look on his face.

"Chrissie," Collin bellowed out with surprise.

Chrissie jumped off Albert's lap and to her feet with a flustered, startled look. She avoided looking at either man and hurried from the room without saying a word. Collin hurried after her and caught up to her in the hallway. He grabbed her arm and forced her to turn and face him.

"What the hell?" he demanded. "You came here with me? Did you forget our deal?"

"No, I didn't forget," she replied sternly and stared into his eyes with some embarrassment but no remorse. "Understand, Collin, I have a shot with Albert Mercer, the richest man this side of anywhere. I'm not passing that up for some measly promotion you could offer."

She stormed off leaving Collin speechless.

✝

Selena soaked in the heavily circulating hot tub on the patio and appeared content and relaxed while the late afternoon sun beat down upon her. Her blonde hair shined like spun gold in the sunlight. Kane studied her from several feet away and allowed his thoughts to stray. He watched her a moment longer then approached with a pleasant smile on his face.

"Mind if I join you?" Kane asked.

Selena jolted from her daze then looked at him and offered a sympathetic smile. "After your day, you need this more than I do," she teased and smiled more naturally than she had the entire week. "How are you feeling?"

Kane removed his shoes and shirt and joined her in the hot tub. As he sat, he groaned softly with severe discomfort. The hot tub felt good but sitting didn't.

"Sore, but I'm blaming that on eight hours on horseback," he teased and weakly grimaced. "I think my cowboy days are just about over."

"At your age, I should think so."

The callousness of her comment hit him. He attempted a smile then looked away so she wouldn't see it bothered him. Perhaps this wasn't working because she felt he was too old for her. It seemed odd that he couldn't think of anything to say to her. He felt they had nothing in common, yet in three years, they were so in love and enjoyed many things together. Their relationship seemed so foreign to him. It was as if he didn't know this woman. He saw Riley approaching the hot tub and couldn't seem to take his eyes off her. Selena saw her as well, immediately frowned, and stood.

"Well, that's my cue--"

He glanced at Selena and appeared surprised. "Are you two still not talking?" Kane asked.

"I'm not talking. She's being a bitch," Selena scoffed and shook her head defiantly. "As if I'd purposely give her a radio that didn't work. I don't know what her problem is, but I'd rather not get into it with her."

Selena left the hot tub, grabbed her towel, and ignored Riley as she passed her. Riley watched Selena leave then looked at Kane in the hot tub and smirked deviously at him.

"Was it something I said?" Riley teased.

Riley removed her shorts and shirt to reveal her conservative bikini. Kane took in her toned body, stared longer than he should, and then immediately tensed while looking away. His body was once again acting inappropriately, and he wasn't sure how to prevent those responses. Casper was right. She was hot, and he couldn't pretend she wasn't. Riley joined him in the hot tub and sat a couple of feet away from him. He avoided looking at her until the water covered her body that taunted him.

"Have you seen Hayes? He disappeared right after dinner," Riley remarked.

"No, I haven't." He considered her comment then muttered, "I hope he didn't go for a walk."

Kane appeared tense and again avoided looking at her. The thought of her kissing him crept back into his mind, and it bothered him. After all, this woman later kills his girlfriend. He was ashamed of his inappropriate thoughts. He was even more ashamed of his arousal to her kiss. He was thankful she hadn't been pressed against him enough to notice that. At least if he was the only one who knew, he could pretend it never happened. Of course, even that was proving difficult. Riley studied him a moment then shifted while looking away.

"I guess Selena's not the only one I'm making uncomfortable these days," Riley remarked and appeared tense as well. She attempted a weak smile, but it was obvious something was bothering her. "You can relax. I'm not going to molest you. I'm not nearly as aggressive as you think."

He stared at her and had to keep from laughing. "No, I think you're more aggressive than you think you are," Kane teased then felt ashamed by the comment and looked away.

His thoughts immediately strayed back to the way she came on to him and kissed him without any warning in the cave. It was actually one of those moments he and Casper loved to tease about in their younger years--or more fondly known as yesterday to his younger self. Things like that never happened to him. Now that they had, his feelings were mixed. Who was he kidding? The thought was making him insane!

Riley grinned in response to his comment. "Considering I've never been with a man, I'd have to say you're wrong."

Kane suddenly looked at her and was surprised by her comment. She'd managed to peak his interest. She was a virgin? "You're kidding, right?" He didn't actually mean to say that aloud but realized it too late. "Is that even possible?"

"I'm going to have to answer 'yes' to that," she remarked while hiding her smile. "Between us--?"

Kane nodded and watched her with a strange anticipation to what she was about to say next. He couldn't believe she was sharing this private information with him. He couldn't believe he wanted to hear more about it.

Riley frowned and suddenly appeared uncomfortable. She took a deep breath and her look turned serious. "When Hayes suggested coming up here, I sort of intended to seduce him." There was an odd silence from both. "I thought it was time I experienced certain *things*, and he was the logical choice." She groaned lowly and rolled her eyes. "Then he suddenly meets someone." Riley avoided looking at Kane while fidgeting. "I guess Selena was right. Obviously, I'm happy for him, but it wasn't the trip I thought it would be."

Kane stared at her and finally put it altogether. Everything suddenly made sense. "That would explain a lot," he accidentally said aloud.

She looked at him and appeared stunned. "Have I been acting that odd?" Riley asked while grimacing.

"No, it's just--" Kane considered then smiled gently. "Just thinking out loud."

"Well, that's my story. What's yours?" She fidgeted slightly possibly at her own directness. "I mean, it's obvious you've been trying to impress Selena," Riley remarked casually. "I've seen the way you look at her. Considering her recent tiff with Tucker, I'd say your odds just increased. I can help, you know. I know what she looks for in men."

"Yeah, a younger one," he muttered.

"Selena doesn't appreciate mature men the way I do," she replied with a tiny smile. "You should be playing the financial security card. Personally, I think you can do better." Riley hesitated possibly regretting having said that aloud. "Selena might be fun for a while, but she's only going to break your heart."

Kane stared at Riley with surprise to the comment, but she was so sincere, he couldn't condemn her for it. She appeared tense then fidgeted while standing. Kane could almost feel Riley's world crashing around her, and he actually felt bad for her. He knew the emotional roller coaster she was riding; it was the same one he'd been on the last week.

"It's been a rough day," she announced a little softer than usual. "If I don't see you in the morning before we checkout, maybe I'll see you around the museum."

Riley walked past Kane and approached the steps. Kane caught her hand as she was about to leave. He wasn't sure why he had done that and didn't even know what it was he intended to say. He just couldn't let her leave feeling the way she did. They exchanged stares in a strange, perplexing silence. He couldn't even guess what his eyes said to her, but it made her smile. Riley kissed him quickly on the lips. Before she could pull away, his hand was on her neck and he returned the kiss with a little too much passion. She eagerly responded. His body reacted so quickly, it almost caused him physical pain. She broke off the kiss, smiled timidly, and left the hot tub. Kane stared after her, took in her toned backside as she walked away, and then groaned lowly while shutting his eyes.

"What the hell is wrong with me?"

Chapter Twenty-eight

Kane walked down the stairs toward the lounge later that evening. It had been an exhausting day, but he couldn't seem to relax. His mind was flooded with thoughts and emotions, some of which were quite troubling. The hot tub didn't help, but that was Riley's fault. That long, hot shower he took afterwards didn't help either. Perhaps a few drinks would relax him. The last thing he needed was a sleepless night watching the clock. He had too many of those in the last week. As he entered the archway to the lounge, he saw Hayes sitting on the sofa with a drink in his hand and a distant look on his face. He appeared to be fighting some particularly nasty demons of his own. Kane studied him and considered if he wanted to get involved in someone else's problems when he had so many of his own. He reluctantly approached Hayes on the sofa and sat in the chair across from him. Hayes didn't even acknowledge that he had entered. Perhaps he hadn't even noticed. Kane studied him a moment before speaking.

"Everything okay?" Kane asked.

Hayes snapped out of his trance, shifted in his seat, and immediately appeared uncomfortable. "That cave-in has me a little unsettled," he said softly and shook his head. "I should have been there. Riley could have been killed."

"She's fine."

"So she keeps saying," he remarked then groaned softly, rolled his eyes shut, and leaned his head against the back of the sofa. "I really screwed up with her, and I don't know how to make it right." He straightened and looked at Kane. "If anything had happened to her--"

"But nothing did."

Hayes' mood didn't improve. Kane sank into thought and carefully considered what he should say. His thoughts strayed to his conversation with Riley in the hot tub, but he couldn't stop thinking about their kiss--their third kiss! He couldn't believe he kissed her back. He couldn't believe how much he enjoyed it! His body ached in agreement. Kane shook the inappropriate thoughts from his mind. It was time to do the right thing.

"I'm going to give you some free advice, Hayes," Kane finally said. "Be honest with her. She knows you've met someone but feels like you're pushing her away."

Hayes stared at him and appeared slightly surprised by his candor. He groaned softly and replied, "It's just so complicated."

"What makes it so complicated?"

Hayes finally looked at him with all seriousness. "I ran into an old friend. We were close once, but she never had romantic feelings for me," he said with a reluctant sigh. The look on his face said it all. "Suddenly, there she was, ravishing me. My head was spinning for days."

Kane stared at him and suddenly felt envious and tense at the same time. "I've never had a woman ravish me," he remarked faintly and wondered what that would be like. He immediately pushed the fantasy out of his head. "You're one lucky man."

"I'm glad you think so," Hayes muttered and remained conflicted. "I don't want to ruin things between Riley and me, but at the same time, I don't want to give up mind-blowing sex several times a day either."

Kane squirmed in his seat and attempted not to grin like a schoolboy, but he was perversely fascinated and it showed. "Several times a day?"

"Oh, yeah," he groaned while playing with his drink. "She just shows up whenever the mood strikes her, makes my head spin, and goes about her day."

"You'd be an idiot to give that up," Kane announced a little louder and a little quicker than he'd intended.

Kane fidgeted in his seat by how he must have sounded. He wanted to entertain that particular fantasy, but attempted to put it out of his head. Even at the height of their erotic moments, Selena had never taken him to that level. In hindsight, that was probably his own fault. Although, he had attempted to seduce her in the antique store afterhours once. That didn't go over as well as he'd anticipated. Kane returned his focus to Hayes' dilemma.

"Talk to Riley," Kane stated. "She's a remarkable young woman."

"She certainly is," Hayes eagerly replied. "I'd gladly spend the rest of my life pining for her."

Kane stared at Hayes. His feelings for his assistant were all too clear. "You love Riley, don't you?" he asked gently.

Hayes didn't even bother looking at him. He just snorted his response as if to say 'no kidding'.

"Maybe you should tell her how you feel," Kane gently informed him.

"I assure you," Hayes announced boldly, "she's aware of my feelings. She's known how I've felt about her for years. It's no secret."

"Maybe," Kane replied. "People change, Hayes. She may surprise you."

He stood with added stiffness, patted Hayes on the shoulder, and left the lounge.

✝

*T*hat evening, Kane sat on the porch and stared at the dark, quiet countryside that seemed to stretch on forever. He'd been thinking about everything, yet thinking about nothing. So many thoughts filled his head, but he couldn't keep a single thought straight. He didn't remember life being this complicated. He loved Selena; he knew he did. It almost seemed troubling that he had to convince himself that he did. This trip to the past had emotionally scarred him. Selena's disinterest was puzzling and actually quite frightening. What made matters worse; every time he attempted to evaluate his relationship with Selena, Riley popped into his head. He couldn't keep her out of his thoughts. He absolutely hated her for killing Selena in the future, but she made it so easy to want her in the past. He chased after Connie in the city nightclub for months before she'd go out with him, and she wouldn't even let him kiss her for a week. Selena let him kiss her on their first date, but they didn't sleep together for nearly three months. Now here he was, he hadn't even been on a date with Riley, and she'd already kissed him three times! Perhaps the universe was punishing him for messing with the timeline. The porch door opened, snapping Kane out of his rant-filled daydream. Selena walked past him, sat on the railing, and smiled at him. He suddenly felt anxious by her presence. Did she know he was thinking about Riley? Was it cheating?

"Well, I don't know what you said to Riley, but I'm back on her good side," Selena informed him.

Kane was surprised by her comment. "I didn't say anything to her."

That didn't make any sense. If Selena were back in Riley's good graces, why would she kill her five years from now? Maybe Casper had it wrong. Maybe he wouldn't be able to return to his own time even if he never had a reason to leave it in the first place. Perhaps he was stuck here for eternity. The thought was sobering. Everything would be ruined. At least for him--this him. The older version of him.

"She says you did. You made quite an impression on her," she informed him in an almost timid tone. "Made me think about what a jerk Tucker was." Selena reflected then smiled. "I'm glad we're through."

"Young men can be immature."

"You're right. I need to have an adult relationship for a change," she announced with a soft sigh. "Maybe Riley has the right idea about mature men."

Kane and Selena stared at each other in silence. Kane wondered if she was saying what he thought she was saying. His heartbeat quickened, but his arousal wasn't there. Perhaps she'd played too many games with his head and now his body needed further reassurances.

Selena flashed a lustful smile while playing with her necklace not far from her low-cut shirt. It almost seemed as if she was attempting to draw attention to her cleavage.

"Know any mature men?" she teased.

"Quite a few, actually," Kane replied while attempting to read her smile and the meaning behind it.

Selena stood, leaned over him, and kissed him warmly but passionately on the mouth. She pulled away and looked into his eyes with the same, lustful smile.

"If you feel like talking, I'll be in my room," she whispered almost seductively.

Selena ran her hand along his chest as she walked passed him and headed inside. Kane appeared stunned, his mouth hanging open, and watched her leave. What the hell just happened? Was she inviting him to her room? It didn't seem possible. They didn't sleep together for nearly three months after they started dating. Did she do some sort of sexual growing in the next three years as well? This hell he was living in made no sense!

Chapter Twenty-nine

*K*ane walked along the second floor hallway only ten minutes after his baffling conversation with Selena and approached one of the guestroom doors. He hesitated before the door and took a deep, nervous breath. He couldn't believe he was doing this. Nothing made sense anymore and trying to sort through it was giving him a headache. Kane gathered all his courage and lightly tapped on the door. He couldn't believe how fast his heart was beating. Why was he so nervous? The door opened to reveal Riley. She stared at him and appeared slightly surprised.

"Kane, is something wrong?" she asked.

"What did you say to Selena?" he suddenly demanded to know while cocking his head sharply to the side. "She invited me to her room to *talk*."

Riley smirked and leaned seductively against the doorframe with her arms folded across her chest. "You're welcome. So why the hell are you here talking to me?"

Kane glared at her and appeared offended. "I don't need your help getting laid." He immediately regretted using that term in mixed company. Apparently, he'd be hanging out with Casper too long.

"Yes, actually, you do," she announced boldly and straightened, allowing her arms to drop to her sides.

He was stunned by her comment.

"It was degrading watching you try to impress Selena while she brushed you off like a speck of dirt. You don't deserve to be treated that way," she remarked sternly then turned almost hostile. "And you're one to preach. Explain Hayes suddenly dropping by to profess his love for me."

Kane was horrified by her callousness. He was concerned about what must have transpired between them. "You didn't shoot him down, did you?" he suddenly demanded.

"What the hell do you think?" she lashed out. "I told you I was happy he found someone, and then you go polluting his mind with the fairy tale of us living happily ever after."

"Will you just listen to yourself?" he suddenly bellowed and felt his irritation building. "You want him. Stop being so damned stubborn and just admit it."

Riley immediately became offended by the comment and took a quick, disgusted step toward him. "I don't want him, you idiot! I want you!"

She tensed to her own words, immediately blushed with embarrassment, and avoided looking at him. Kane stared at her with surprise as a thousand confusing thoughts exploded in his mind. His body twitched in response.

"I'm sorry," she said with a frown while finally able to make eye contact. "That's the tequila talking."

Kane stared at her a long moment and attempted to organize his racing thoughts. "Riley, I--"

His sudden arousal was stronger than anything he'd ever felt before, and his need to act upon it swept over him in a wild rush of sexual desire. Kane suddenly groaned, pulled her into his arms, and kissed her passionately. Riley hesitated only a moment then returned the kiss with an aggression he'd never experienced before. She pulled him into the room without breaking off the kiss and closed the door behind him. She half pulled him to the bed and attempted to undress him without a single hesitation. He aggressively lowered her to the bed while firmly running his hands along her body. She kissed him passionately and aggressively, which only increased his own aggression. They shed their clothing without missing a beat. Kane's head was spinning as Riley responded to every touch and every kiss with more passion then he ever thought possible. What should have been an awkward first time wasn't awkward at all. As with every conversation he'd ever had with her, she was making their sexual encounter too easy for him. Her every response filled him with increasing confidence that he could do no wrong. He attempted to slow things down when the thought of her being a virgin echoed through his mind, but she continued to encourage him and showed no resistance or apprehension. It was as if she wanted him to show aggression! He couldn't take much more then finally gave in to the temptation and proceeded more aggressively. He hoped he wasn't being too aggressive, but she wasn't resisting--only encouraging. He couldn't remember the last time he'd felt so sexually invigorated. He felt almost drunk while making love to Riley. The insanely wild moment finally passed, and he panted heavily while motionless on top of her. Reality flooded back to him, and he looked into her eyes for any indication that he hadn't been too aggressive with her. He feared he might have hurt her with his animal like behavior. He didn't know what came over him. Riley clung to him and caressed his lower back while rubbing her calves against his naked buttocks. Her lustful grin told him everything he wanted to know. He smiled and kissed her warmly and with less aggression and more passion.

"I could happily do that all night," she cooed softly while firmly caressing his body.

Kane groaned his pleasure to her comment and kissed her warmly. "Be careful, I may take you up on that offer." The thought was arousing.

"I'd be disappointed if you didn't," she remarked softly then giggled.

Kane's entire body twitched to the comment, and after a small breather, he intended to test her on that. He moved off her and immediately pulled her into his arms. Riley was nestled against Kane beneath the sheets while clinging to him. He held her to his chest and remained out of breath but smiling. Riley appeared pleasantly rumpled and pleased while running her hand firmly along his chest. He attempted to look at her while hiding his boyish grin. It almost didn't seem possible for sex to be that exhilarating, especially considering she was--

Kane's brows knitted as he looked at her while she nuzzled against him. "Are you sure you were a virgin?"

"I don't have a doctor's note, if that's what you mean," she teased.

"No, I'll take your word for it. I just wasn't expecting you to be quite so *aggressive*."

"I may be guilty of watching one or two training videos," she teased. "A girl should come prepared."

Kane was surprised by the comment then laughed softly and shook his head. He held her firmly against his naked body. "You're nothing like I expected."

"What were you expecting?"

He considered her question then chuckled almost humored by it. "Someone else."

Kane only allowed his thoughts to stray for a moment. As Selena entered his mind, he easily dismissed any thoughts of her, rolled Riley onto her back, and lovingly kissed her.

†

Selena walked along the second floor hallway just a little before ten o'clock that evening. She appeared disgusted as she approached Riley's bedroom door. It was obvious her evening hadn't gone according to her plans. She was about to knock when she heard voices within the room. Riley's giggles were followed by Kane's low, soft voice. Selena lowered her hand from the door and stared at it with apparent surprise.

"I don't believe it," Selena gasped softly.

Her look conveyed her irritation and possible embarrassment after offering herself to Kane. She stormed away from the room and hurried down the stairs. Selena nearly collided with Hayes at the bottom of the stairs, startling both.

"You're certainly in a hurry," Hayes announced then grinned teasingly. "Are they serving margaritas on the promenade deck?" He'd obviously had a few drinks and was feeling little pain.

Selena appeared flustered, hesitated only a moment, and then held her head proudly. "No, I just had a near embarrassing moment," she informed him. "I went to Riley's room to see if she wanted to soak in the hot tub tonight. Thank God, I didn't knock. She's *entertaining* someone."

Hayes' expression shattered as he stared at Selena and the strange smirk on her face. She seemed a little too eager to share her findings with him.

"She's *with* someone?" he asked as his voice cracked. The look on his face was wildly unpredictable and most certainly conveyed jealousy.

"I can only assume it was Kane," Selena informed him. "I've seen the way she's been looking at him lately. She was just telling me about his successful antique store."

Hayes didn't even appear to be paying attention to her now. He stared blankly at the floor with his brows heavily knitted. She studied him with concern.

"Are you okay, Hayes?"

He suddenly looked up at her and fumbled for something to say. "Uh, yes, I'm fine."

Selena placed her hand on his lower arm and smiled sweetly. "I'm sorry I said anything. I wasn't thinking. You're obviously upset," she said gently. "Why don't we have a drink? We can talk about it."

He stared at her a moment, snapped out of his trance, and shook his head. "No, thank you. I think I'm just going to go to my room and read a little. Good night, Selena."

Hayes hurried up the stairs. Only a moment passed before his door was heard slamming. Selena frowned with disgust and folded her arms across her chest. Collin appeared on the stairs and approached her on the first floor. He pointed up the stairs with a dumbfounded expression.

"What was that about?" Collin asked.

Selena shrugged. "Beats me," she said with a sigh. "Seems like everyone is turning in early tonight. Not even any television. I'm already bored out of my mind."

"Yeah, me too," Collin replied with a defeated sigh. "Want to join me for a drink?"

She shrugged while frowning. "Why not? I don't have anything else to do tonight."

✝

*L*ater that night, sometime after midnight, Collin walked along the second floor hallway while playing with his old-fashioned, brass room key. He appeared intoxicated and proud of it. A guestroom door opened behind him and raised voices were heard. Collin turned and looked back down the hall. Albert shoved a partially dressed Chrissie into the hallway. She clung to her clothes while arguing with him.

"What the hell--?" she exploded. "That's it?"

"What were you expecting?" Albert demanded. "I'm tired, and I want to sleep."

"But I don't have a room--"

"Too bad," Albert replied and hid his smirk. "You're not sleeping here."

The door shut almost in her face. Chrissie stared at the closed door with a look of astonishment and possible horror. She then looked down the hall and saw Collin staring at her in her undergarments while clinging to her bundled clothing. She frowned shamefully and approached him.

"Sorry, Chrissie," he announced while shaking his head. "You made your bed." He then grinned drunkenly. "Pity you don't have one to lie in."

Collin snickered and headed for his room, leaving Chrissie alone and half-naked in the hallway.

Chapter Thirty

Casper stood before the small check in desk within the lobby the following morning and handed his brass room key to Bessie, who sat behind the desk. She smiled warmly at him, and they exchanged a few pleasantries.

"I enjoyed your company," Bessie said to Casper. "I get a lot of guests, but none quite like you."

"Yeah, I'm one of a kind," he teased. "One of me is enough."

"Well, I think you're sweet," she said warmly. "Don't ever change."

"I doubt I ever will," he replied.

Kane suddenly approached and pulled him away from the desk with amazing force, startling the large man. Bessie watched with surprise as well.

"Dude!"

Kane pulled Casper across the room out of earshot of the innkeeper and forced him to face him. The look on Kane's face was desperate. "I need your help. I'm in big trouble."

Casper's eyes widened with horror. "You didn't kill anyone, did you?"

"What? No!" Kane fidgeted and was unable to stand still. "I sort of slept with Riley last night."

"Dude!" he exclaimed with a grin.

Kane quickly looked around the room with embarrassment. "Will you keep it down!"

"Relax," Casper announced while chuckling. "I already told you it doesn't matter. You'll be returned to the future like it never happened." He then appeared to consider and was less convinced. "On the other hand, Riley may be a little pissed when *you* start dating Selena in three years, and the *you* that I know won't remember having slept with her. That might be a little awkward. Women tend to get upset by things like that."

"That's not the problem, Casper."

"Sounds like one to me," Casper muttered and thought about the situation. "That girl could put a serious hurting on you. You know, the *you* that's here." He groaned while rolling his eyes and shook his head. "Man, the *you* here has no idea what sort of trouble you're causing for him."

Kane couldn't take much more of Casper's mindless chatter. "Casper, I want to be with Riley," he said firmly then tensed. "I think I'm falling in love with her."

Casper appeared excited. "Dude!" He suddenly frowned and reconsidered his initial enthusiasm. "There's no way to make that work. If Riley doesn't kill Selena, you don't time travel, and you'll return to the future and marry Selena. The only way you can stay here is if Riley kills Selena, in which case she becomes a snarling, nasty beast."

"There has to be a way," Kane protested. "What if I come clean with Riley?"

"Providing she doesn't think you're totally insane, you're still going to return to the future if Selena doesn't die. There's no way for you to be with Riley." Casper placed a hand on Kane's shoulder. "The only practical solution is for you to keep Hayes from being killed and return to your life. Trust me, you won't even remember Riley," he gently informed him. "In three years, you'll fall in love with Selena. It'll all work out."

"That's not the answer I was looking for," Kane muttered while frowning.

"Sorry, dude," Casper replied. "It's not possible."

Kane felt defeated, groaned with disgust, and walked away from his friend. "I need some air."

†

*K*ane walked along the well-groomed path in the woods and remained completely distracted. He wasn't sure how long he'd been walking, but it had to be an hour or more. Life seemed so unfair. He knew he was being ridiculous. Casper was right. In three years, he was going to fall in love with Selena and the world would be as it should. He'd never even remember his feelings for Riley. He'd never remember that he loved. The thought made his stomach tie in knots. He attempted to collect his thoughts and focus on what he could control. Right now, today, Hayes was still in danger, and that needed to be his first priority. Thoughts of Riley continued to haunt him. Last night was possibly the greatest sex of his life. He cursed himself for even thinking something like that. It was disrespectful to Selena. He attempted to think about how wonderful life was going to be once he saved Selena from certain death. They were going to be married; and life would be wonderful. Kane suddenly cursed himself. It was no use; he just couldn't keep Riley out of his head! Why did sex have to be so incredible with her last night? He stopped by the washed out trail and stared at the rocky crevice. It took him a few seconds to realize he was staring at the exact spot where Hayes was supposed to have died yesterday. He looked up then down the slope. The rocks hadn't fallen! How was that possible? Kane appeared puzzled then alarmed. It wasn't an accident! The rocks hadn't fallen because Hayes hadn't made the hike! He turned and ran back toward the inn. Kane ran for what seemed a long time before finally appearing in the clearing surrounding the inn. He ran for the porch where Casper impatiently sat on one of the rocking chairs and waited for him with an annoyed look on his face.

"Where have you been?" Casper demanded. "Everyone else left."

"We need to talk," Kane announced while out of breath and drenched in sweat. "I'm going to take a quick shower, grab my bag, and meet you here in thirty minutes."

"Sure, why not?" Casper scoffed. "I have nothing better to do."

Kane hurried inside.

Casper casually rocked in the chair and made a face. "It's not as if I have a job or a boss who's going to fire my ass," he muttered and propped his chin on his fist.

Chapter Thirty-one

Kane appeared from the bathroom freshly showered in his green boxer briefs while carrying his travel kit. He was in the process of hurriedly packing between getting dressed. A thousand thoughts rushed through his mind. The rockslide that didn't happen was top on his list. Despite his attempts to focus, his dilemma with Riley kept creeping back in his mind to haunt him. There was a knock on the door, which wasn't surprising. He was late checking out and would probably be socked with a late checkout fee. He tossed his travel kit into his bag.

"Yeah, I'm checking out in ten minutes," Kane called to the door. It was the last thing on his mind, and he didn't feel like being bothered with something so trivial.

"Kane, it's me," Riley announced through the door.

Kane appeared surprised to hear her voice. His heart immediately skipped a beat. He grinned lustfully and hurried for the door. She hadn't left! She'd waited for him! He couldn't believe how excited just hearing her voice made him. As he bounded for the door, he wondered how inappropriate suggesting a quickie would be. He opened the door to reveal Scarred Riley from the future. His expression suddenly dropped. She kicked him in the chest with her black booted foot, harshly throwing him backwards and across the room. Scarred Riley entered the room and casually locked the door

151

behind her. Kane caught his balance, rubbed his sore bare chest, and stared at her with horror. His horror immediately turned to anger as he stared at the woman in the black stalking outfit.

"You!"

Scarred Riley spun into a kick and struck him in the abdomen. She kicked again and hit him in the shoulder. He was thrown backward onto the bed with a bounce. Scarred Riley jumped on top of him, pinned both his wrists to the bed, and roughly planted her knee between his legs against his crotch. The fact that he only wore his boxer briefs allowed the firmness of her knee to be easily felt against his sensitive areas. She hovered over him while he stared at her scarred face and blind eye with horror. Any anger he'd felt was quickly replaced with fear. The location of her knee assured that. Her look was enraged.

"You son-of-a-bitch!" she growled with a harsh look he couldn't describe. "Do you have any idea what you've done?"

"What I've done?"

Scarred Riley's knee pressed firmly against his crotch. Kane gasped with surprise and discomfort. He attempted to relax her enough to ease pressure on his crotch.

"Okay!" he cried out in a higher pitch than he had been shooting for. "Just relax your knee, please!"

Scarred Riley released pressure from his crotch but kept her knee snug against him. Her knee against his private parts didn't comfort him any but at least his life stopped flashing before his eyes. She maintained her harsh glare while hovering over him only inches from his face.

"I don't know what you're up to, but if you screw things up," she snarled, "I'm going to put you in the ground right alongside your bitch of a girlfriend."

Kane appeared momentarily angered, accessed his situation, and quickly collected himself. Having his nuts bashed in wasn't going to accomplish anything. Even the thought hurt.

"I was only trying to keep Hayes alive," he protested while unable to look away from the woman he loathed.

"Don't play stupid, Kane," she snarled. "I'm talking about what you did to *me* last night."

Kane was suddenly horrified while staring at her. "Oh, God," he gasped and nearly choked on his own words. "Please don't tell me *you* have those memories."

"What? No!" she snarled.

Scarred Riley gracefully jumped off him and the bed. His heart finally stopped pounding, although his testicles had apparently vacated the scene.

"You are so pathetic, you know that?" she scoffed and paced the room like a panther.

Kane quickly sat up and attempted to stand. She glared sharply at him, instantly forcing him back into a sitting position with just a look.

"Yes, I'm probably almost as pathetic as you are," he snapped then immediately regretted saying it aloud.

Kane needed to save the macho talk for when he had the means to back it up. And sitting there in his underwear didn't qualify. Scarred Riley glared at him. Kane tensed but didn't look away. For some reason, he couldn't look away. Scarred Riley groaned softly and shook her head.

"Why did you do it? Some sick revenge on me?" she snarled lowly.

"No, of course not. You--she--" He groaned softly and raked his fingers through his hair. "I doubt I can say anything that won't get my nuts cracked."

Scarred Riley sat on the bed alongside Kane. He jumped with surprise and placed his hand over his crotch. Oddly enough, he was now suddenly aware he was sitting next to her in nothing but his underwear. The fact that they were emerald green didn't make him feel any better.

"I saw you. I saw you standing over me--over Riley with that knife the other night," she informed him. "You intended to kill her."

"You saw that? How--?" Kane took a deep breath and attempted to remain calm in his current predicament. He didn't need to prolong her visit by asking too many questions. "Then you also know I couldn't do it."

"Yes, and if you had tried, you'd be dead," she remarked without emotion. "I was standing in the closet not five feet from you. I could've snapped your neck without even waking my younger counterpart."

Her comment sent a chill down his spine. "I made a mistake, and I'm sorry. I shouldn't have slept with you, uh, her. I just wanted to keep Hayes from dying so you wouldn't kill Selena. I never meant to fall in love--" Kane groaned and held his head. "God, I really screwed things up."

"Yes, and once I figure out what the hell you did, I'll fix it," she informed him with detest in her eyes. "We'll both be returned to the future, and you can marry that whore, Selena."

Scarred Riley abruptly stood and walked toward the door. Kane watched her, allowing his eyes to fall to her backside in the black, slinking outfit she wore. His mind momentarily strayed. Technically, he had his way with that last night and thoughts of a lustful position flooded his mind. He suddenly cursed himself for even thinking such thoughts with that horrible woman. She wasn't Riley. Scarred Riley paused by the door and hesitated with her back turned to him. Kane watched her closely and tried to assess her mood. Was it possible that she somehow had access to those memories? For a moment, he was positive he was dead.

"You can't trust her," she said softly. For a moment, she sounded less like the 'she devil' and more like Riley. "She's not the woman you think she is."

"What are you talking about?"

Scarred Riley turned to face him and frowned. "Selena was only dating you for your money."

He stared at her with surprise and disbelief to her words. He immediately became defensive and possibly hostile. "No, you're wrong. She loved me. We were getting married until you showed up and murdered her."

All glimmer of Riley suddenly vanished, and the hostility of Scarred Riley returned. "She was using you and fucking Tucker behind your back." Her words cut deep. "You may never believe me or even forgive me, but I did you a favor."

"There's no way she was seeing him," Kane announced firmly. "She loved me."

Scarred Riley shook her head with disgust. "I don't know why I even bothered. I knew you wouldn't listen to me, that's why I had to confront her on my own. I should have known you'd show up here and try to ruin everything."

Kane suddenly thought of something he hadn't until that moment. "How did you get here?" he suddenly asked. "You saw me vanish, didn't you?" He suddenly felt pangs of horror as his body twitched. "What did you do to Casper after I traveled back in time?"

"I didn't do anything to him," she scoffed while folding her arms across her chest. "He tried to take off with that trinket box and didn't get ten feet before I pounced on him. He dropped it and took off like a frightened bunny." She smirked deviously. "Fortunately, I know Latin."

His expression suddenly dropped. "You weren't *following* me from the future. You traveled back in time to save Hayes," Kane suddenly announced and quickly put it altogether. "Does he know you're here?"

Scarred Riley stared at him with no emotion.

Kane's eyes widened and his mouth fell open with astonishment. "Oh, God, you're the one he's been seeing!"

Her anger quickly returned. "You're going to stay out of my life, Kane. I'm in love with Hayes and my younger counterpart is going to be with him. It was meant to be."

"She's not in love with him."

"She is; she just doesn't know it yet," she announced sternly. "It took Hayes' death for me to realize how I felt about him. You're going to let this happen, or make no mistake; I *will* take you out of the timeline."

Scarred Riley again turned to leave.

Kane jumped off the bed. "Wait--"

Scarred Riley spun around and glared at him. Kane jumped back with alarm to her sudden movement and reconsidered his actions. He attempted to remain calm, so she wouldn't inflict more pain upon him. He defensively held his hands up to keep her from reacting, but he really wanted to defend his crotch from bodily harm.

"Maybe we can't agree on Riley's fate, but we both want to keep Hayes from dying. Let me help."

"I don't need your help."

"The rockslide never happened," he blurted out. "It wasn't an accident. That's why we're still here."

"I know. Hayes' life is still in danger. I thought I took care of it, but I was wrong," Scarred Riley informed him.

Kane uncertainly lowered his hands and was puzzled by her words. "What do you mean?"

Scarred Riley approached Kane. He tensed slightly but forced himself to stand firm. Her eyes briefly strayed to his green boxer briefs. For some reason, it sent panic through him. He was positive she was looking for an excuse to bash his nuts in.

"Tucker created the rockslide," she informed him. "I suspect he also rigged the mine to blow as a contingency plan."

"Tucker?" Kane gasped with surprise. "Are you sure?"

"He was dressed in camouflage from head to toe, but it was him, I assure you," she informed him. "I ambushed him on the ledge above the rockslide where he was waiting. He didn't know Hayes hadn't shown up."

"But you didn't actually see his face?"

"It was him," she hissed with irritation to the question. "He took off before I could lay him out. He must come back later to finish the job."

"But if I'm still here, you must still blame Selena for whatever happens later," he protested. "There must be something we're missing."

Her hostility again returned. "Let's get this straight, Kane. There is no 'we' in this. You and your little green man panties are going to take a hike."

Kane was startled by the underwear comment but stood firm and sneered back at her. "Until Hayes' life is out of danger, we're both stuck here." He felt phantom pain in his groin. Surprisingly, she made no attempt to harm him.

"You want to hang around?" she snarled. "Fine. But you keep it in your pants. If you do anything to ruin my plans, I'll be paying a call to your younger self at that antique store and perform a homemade castration on him." She cast a look at his crotch that chilled him and sharply raised her brows. "Do we understand each other?"

Kane stared at her with alarm. He was sure she'd do it too. "Yeah, painfully so."

"I'll be in touch."

Scarred Riley casually left the room.

Kane groaned and fell onto the bed while holding his head. "Hayes, you're one brave man to screw that shrew."

Chapter Thirty-two

Two days later. Kane walked across the museum lobby and toward the front desk where Chrissie and Jillian gossiped softly. He'd avoided the museum for the last two days while Casper attempted to formulate a plan based on what Scarred Riley had told him about Tucker possibly being the one threatening Hayes' life. Collin and Noble approached the front desk from the opposite direction. They were softly arguing about something. Whatever their spat, it ended with Noble storming off. As Collin stopped by the desk, the mood suddenly turned hostile, causing Kane to stop in his tracks. Chrissie began shouting at Collin about some incident at the inn. Selena suddenly appeared alongside Kane and watched the display with less interest.

"Looks like someone's trying to lose her job," Selena muttered to Kane.

He briefly glanced at her then looked back at the front desk. Chrissie and Collin were in a soft shouting match while attempting to keep their voices down. Jillian casually stood nearby and listened while pretending she wasn't.

"What happened?" Kane asked.

"Apparently," Selena announced while lustfully raising her brows, "Collin had brought Chrissie along for 'happy hour', but she ditched him for a shot at Albert."

"Albert Mercer? Are you serious?" Kane asked and grimaced with distaste.

"Yeah," she replied and giggled.

"I'll bet that went over well," Kane muttered.

"With Mercer maybe but certainly not with Collin," Selena informed him. "Unfortunately, Chrissie found out that Albert just wanted a quickie, and she hadn't won the lottery after all. Now they're ready to kill each other."

"I guess that little expedition was a bust all the way around, huh?"

"No kidding," Selena announced with a defeated sigh. "Even Hayes and Riley have been feuding. I wonder what possibly could have triggered that." She attempted to hide her devious smile. Selena finally turned toward him, gave him an approving once over, and smiled sweetly. "So where have you been hiding? I haven't seen you since we left the inn."

"I, uh, had business to attend to at my store in the city," Kane remarked.

He felt oddly guilty, as if he had cheated on Selena with Riley. Perhaps he had. He didn't know for sure. It was too complicated. He hoped Casper was right about not remembering any of this. Unfortunately, Riley and Selena both would. The thought wasn't helping settle his anxiety.

"I'd love to see your shop sometime," she remarked while grinning lustfully. "Maybe you could take me there. I'd love to get away from here for a while. A weekend in the city sounds like a lot of fun."

Kane stared at Selena with a strange look. Her sudden interest in him after nearly a week was troubling. And what was with the sudden sexual innuendos? What happened to the good little girl who made him wait three months? Had Riley been right? Was Selena only interested in financially secure men? That couldn't be the case. She never made a big deal about money. Of course, after buying the store from his parents, he never really had much money, so it couldn't be true.

"Yeah, maybe we'll do that," he uncertainly replied. "Is Hayes around?"

"He's been hiding in his office all morning," she announced with little interest then became enthused. "Want to grab some lunch? I get my lunch break in an hour."

"I'm going to be tied up with Hayes for a while. Maybe another time." He couldn't believe he'd just brushed off Selena. He couldn't believe Riley was still clouding his mind.

"Yeah, sure," she replied with a tiny, defeated smile.

Kane felt oddly awkward around her. As he stood before the woman he intended to marry, he couldn't stop thinking about Riley. He hurried away from Selena to escape the guilt and headed toward the offices. He felt guilty enough without her suddenly taking an interest in him, but he couldn't think about that right now. Kane walked along the corridor in the direction of Hayes' office. Hayes stood in the hallway while talking to Riley and seemingly brushed her off. The tension between them was so powerful, Kane felt the ripple affect down the hall. Hayes returned to his office and closed the door. Riley was obviously bothered by the brush off, which was indicated by the sneer on her face. She turned, saw Kane, and appeared even less friendly. She briskly walked past him without making eye contact.

"Kane--" Riley scoffed.

He hurried after her. "Riley, wait."

She didn't stop and avoided looking at or speaking to him. Kane walked alongside her despite her reluctance to acknowledge him and kept stride with her.

"Please, Riley, I just want to talk."

"We don't have anything to talk about," she bluntly informed him.

"The other night--"

"What? Our one-night stand?" Riley interrupted without looking at him.

Kane suddenly caught her arm and forced her to face him. "That's not what it was."

Riley glared at his hand holding her arm then looked into his eyes. There was a hint of Scarred Riley lurking just behind her eyes. Kane nervously released her arm.

"There is absolutely nothing between us," Riley informed him. "Your silence the last two days made that clear."

"I'm sorry about that." He hesitated and considered Scarred Riley's threat. "Believe me; I had two very good reasons for staying away."

"Save it," she scoffed. "I have no one to blame but myself, but that doesn't mean I want to talk to you."

Riley walked away. Kane groaned and leaned against the wall. What the hell happened? He screwed up with Selena; he screwed up with Riley; and he was still no closer to resolving why Riley would later want to kill her former friend. Former friend? Is that how he saw Selena? Riley's former friend; not his fiancé? He heard a familiar male voice from down the hall.

"Did you want to see me or just upset my assistant?" Hayes said from his office doorway.

Kane looked down the hall at Hayes, who casually leaned in the doorframe. Kane approached and appeared defeated.

"I think we should talk," Kane said.

Hayes indicated his office. Kane frowned and entered with Hayes following. Kane suddenly stopped within the office and stared at Scarred Riley sitting seductively on the edge of Hayes' desk. She glared at him with the hatred visible in her eyes. Hayes shut and locked the door behind them then casually returned to his chair behind the desk.

"I believe you've met my girlfriend--"

"Our paths have crossed a couple of times; each more unpleasant than the last," Kane remarked then glared at Scarred Riley. "You told me to stay away from Riley, and I did. She hates me. I hope you're happy."

"She'll get over it. Hayes will make it all better," Scarred Riley remarked with a twisted smile.

Kane glared at Hayes. "So that's the plan? Take advantage of the young woman who admires you?"

Hayes sneered his displeasure to the comment. "I love Riley. I would never do anything to hurt her," he remarked and held up his head proudly. "I'll continue to wait for her."

Scarred Riley appeared alarmed, sprang off the desk, and turned to face him. "No, you need to make your move now. Vulnerable or not, it's what she needs. You already let that one--" she indicated Kane "--slip past you and into her bed."

Kane was almost amused by what he was witnessing. At least he wasn't the only one under her whip. "Oh, so I'm not the only one she's dominating," he remarked with a smirk. "What happened, Hayes? She verbally castrate you too?"

Scarred Riley glared at Kane and took a step toward him. "You want to play, Kane? I'll play."

"That's enough from both of you," Hayes announced while standing then looked at Kane. "I didn't ask for this, but when the woman you've loved as long as you can remember suddenly shows up and gives you hope, you can't say no."

"Yes, you were given what you've always wanted, but she's not Riley," Kane said firmly and glared at Scarred Riley. "She's the byproduct of your death. She's so badly damaged that she murders

Selena out of revenge. You may see the woman you love, but I see a cold-blooded killer."

Scarred Riley sneered at Kane.

"You see what you want to see, Kane," Hayes replied with little reaction.

"No, *you* see what you want to see. The woman you've been screwing has been out of your life for five years," Kane informed him and gave her a loathing once over. "God knows what evil she's done in that time." He straightened proudly and shook his head with conviction. "That's not Riley."

"I don't care who she is. I love her."

Scarred Riley looked at Hayes and smiled warmly for the first time. For a brief moment, she seemed almost human. Hayes pulled her into his arms. They held each other in a loving embrace. Hayes kissed her warmly on the lips then nodded toward the door. Scarred Riley smiled, put on a baseball cap and sunglasses, and slipped from the office. Hayes' eyes remained on her until she was gone. He casually sat on the edge of his desk, inhaled deeply, and looked at Kane.

"I know what you must think of me, but if it wasn't for Riley, today would be my funeral," Hayes informed him. "She came back for me, because she loves me. Isn't that why you came back to save Selena?"

"She came back to save you, because her life fell apart after you died," he informed him. "Your relationship with young Riley isn't going to change."

"No, not when she has you in her life to complicate things," Hayes remarked.

"I know it's in her best interest that I stay away," Kane announced and attempted to hide the pain in his voice. "There's nothing I can do to keep her, I've already conceded to that, but that woman sharing your bed is poisoning your mind." He stared at Hayes with a serious look. "I know what she is."

"You think she's the monster who murdered your girlfriend," Hayes remarked simply then raised his brows with conviction. "She said it was self-defense. She told me she went there to confront Selena. It was Selena who pulled the gun and tried to kill her--not the other way around."

"Selena wouldn't do that," he interjected and tried to control his quickly rising temper. "Where would she have gotten a gun? She's never even fired one."

"Ironic that you're so confident about Selena, yet when you had the opportunity, you chose to sleep with Riley instead of the woman you say you love. You may claim that woman isn't Riley, but I know Riley better than you do." He hesitated while staring at Kane and cleverly raised his brows. "Something tells me I probably know Selena better too."

"So what's the big plan? You just continue getting it on with Miss Personality until she thwarts your killer then move on to the next Riley?" Kane asked.

"Wasn't that sort of like your plan? Bang my Riley until you're sent back to marry Selena?" Hayes asked. His crude sexual reference conveyed his true feelings about what happened between Kane and Riley at the inn.

"She's not your Riley."

"Yes, she is my Riley," he growled, stood abruptly, and turned defensive. "I love her and I'd do anything for her." The look in Hayes' eyes was wild and unpredictable. "You, on the other hand, came here for Selena. I'm starting to think you two deserve each other."

Kane was frustrated with the entire conversation. It was obvious neither was about to back down. "That's not important right now," he announced. "I'm still here, which means nothing has changed. If what Riley said is true, Tucker must come back to finish what he started."

"I'm aware of the situation," Hayes replied simply. "Riley told me everything. She's going to remain close by and keep watch for Tucker. I'm confident she'll eliminate the threat. In case you hadn't noticed, she's quite *skilled*."

"Yes," Kane muttered and hid his sneer. "I've witnessed her talent for destruction firsthand. I'll admit, I would have been impressed if it hadn't been for the fact that she'd just murdered my girlfriend, and I was writhing around the floor in total agony from the experience."

"You paint an interesting and unique picture," Hayes remarked then shook his head and smirked as if hiding some secret from the man before him. "Ask yourself one question, Kane. If she's such a monster, why did she let you live? Don't pretend it hasn't crossed your mind. Once you answer that question, everything will make sense, I promise."

"I have asked myself that question," Kane replied. "I've concluded that she's easily amused, and I wasn't worth her effort. Now you need to ask yourself a question." Kane casually stood and stared at the man before him. "Which Riley do you want more? The young, innocent one who thinks of you as her best friend? Or the temptress seducing you with mind-blowing sex several times a day?"

Hayes stared at Kane and appeared almost bewildered by the question. Kane smirked and headed for the office door. He paused by the door and turned to face Hayes.

"I'll catch up with you later," Kane announced then grinned. "We'll compare answers then." He opened the door and left.

Chapter Thirty-three

*K*ane stood partially hidden near the entrance to the mummy exhibit and stared across the massive, mostly finished room. Hayes and Riley worked on a display while joking around. Apparently, they'd worked things out from their earlier disagreement. Hayes hugged Riley and appeared reluctant to let her go. She didn't seem to mind being in his arms. Their feelings for each other were stronger than most married couple's feelings. Maybe Scarred Riley had been right. Perhaps Riley just needed a push in the right direction. Had he nearly ruined something with which he never should have been involved? He couldn't be with her anyway. Perhaps it was for the best. Kane frowned. All his questions were leaving him with a massive headache and a lump in his throat. He turned to leave before they became aware of his presence and nearly collided with Scarred Riley, who stood alongside him. Her attention was focused on Hayes with her younger self. Her sudden and silent appearance frightened him. She cast a glance at him and raised her brows.

"I know you're not entertaining any wild thoughts," Scarred Riley casually remarked.

"Just leave me alone," Kane scoffed and headed into the next exhibit to put some distance between them.

As Kane walked through the dinosaur exhibit, Scarred Riley casually followed him. Kane attempted to ignore her taunting presence, but it was obvious she wasn't about to let him off the hook so easily. She was too much like a cat stalking its prey. He was certain she would enjoy watching him squirm while she sank her claws into him as well. Why did he suddenly hate cats?

"It's nothing personal, you know," she informed him with a casual tone that conveyed her arrogance. "Everything is going to play out as it was meant to. You'll be back with that bitch, Selena, get married, and have a few good months before they whack you for your grandmother's inheritance."

Kane suddenly stopped and turned to face her with a strange look of surprise. "How did you know about my inheritance?"

"Oh, Kane, you just don't get it," Scarred Riley said with a sigh while folding her arms across her chest. "I told you about Tucker and Selena. I followed them. I listened to them plan and plot against you."

"Hayes said you killed Selena in self-defense," he announced then sneered. "I find that difficult to believe."

Scarred Riley approached Kane, casually placed her arms around his neck, and looked into his eyes with only a few inches between their faces. Despite her intimidating appearance, her closeness suddenly didn't seem to bother him. Pangs of sexual desire from his night with her younger counterpart throbbed within his entire body. He was seeing her beyond the scar and blind eye. He wanted her; and it frightened him.

"Look at me. I can beat the crap out of grown men twice my size," she informed him with a seductive almost playful grin. Her fingers gently ran along the back of his neck, sending a ripple of desire through his body. "Do you think I'd need a gun to confront a little shit like Selena? I could snap her like a twig."

Kane stared into Scarred Riley's eyes, despite the blind one. She may have been Riley's evil twin; but she was still Riley. He resisted the urge to pull her into his arms and forced himself to keep his hands firmly at his sides. He was stronger than that! She wasn't going to play him.

"So you expect me to believe you just went to confront Selena on my behalf?" he snorted softly and smirked while shaking his head. "That you weren't seeking revenge for Hayes? You must really think I'm an idiot."

Scarred Riley appeared tense. She allowed her hands to slip from his shoulders and firmly along his chest before taking a step back. Her hands traveling his chest sent shockwaves through his body. It bothered him that it didn't bother him. His thoughts slipped back to that night at the inn when he made mad, passionate love to her multiple times. Kane's body suddenly tensed. It wasn't this woman! Why was he thinking such things? She remained uncomfortably close, and his body wasn't about to let him forget her closeness. The look on her face was once again reminiscing of her younger self, making it difficult for Kane to distinguish between the two.

"I didn't want to see Selena hurt you the way she'd hurt me. They tried to erase my emotions, but I didn't lose them all," she said almost softly then turned cold. "When our lives return to the way they were meant to be, I won't interfere with your relationship. I'll be happily married to Hayes, and you'll have to watch your own back."

He stared at her and suddenly tilted his head in question. "Who are *they*?"

"Excuse me?" she asked.

"You said *they* tried to erase your emotions," he announced while staring at her. "Who are *they*?"

"Where else would an angry young woman go? To her uncle's mercenary friends. I asked for their help, and they put me through training most men wouldn't survive," Scarred Riley announced then grinned. "Just the finishing touches on the well-mannered woman standing before you today."

"They accomplished their goal. I think you're both intimidating and frightening," Kane remarked. "Although he'd never admit it, I'm sure Hayes fears for his testicles too."

"Well, we can't all have virgins, now can we?" she snapped. Despite her emotionless expression, her body twitched in response. She was obviously bothered that he got to her younger counterpart first. "In my reality, I gave that up to a couple of mercenaries on a daily basis as payment for my training."

Kane stared at her with surprise then shut his eyes almost painfully and looked away. "I'm sorry, Riley."

She suddenly snorted a laugh. "Why? We all got what we wanted, and it was a learning experience like anything else," she informed him. "It's not as if I was forced to do anything I didn't want to do."

"I can't imagine Riley going through what you had," he said softly while staring at her with an unusual tenderness. "You may refuse to admit it, but what happened between me and Riley makes you a part of me as well."

Scarred Riley appeared bewildered; although it was possible she was contemplating striking him. Despite his concerns, Kane refused to back down. He placed his hand to her face and gently caressed the scar on her cheek.

"I'm so sorry I hurt you," he whispered softly.

Scarred Riley stared into his eyes, and, for a moment, he wasn't certain how she was going to react. She suddenly kissed him passionately and aggressively on the mouth. Kane appeared startled and considered pushing her away, but changed his mind and returned the aggressive kiss. He was immediately reminded of the intense night of passion he shared with young Riley, and he didn't want to give it up. The lights suddenly went out. Scarred Riley broke off the kiss and jumped away from him. They looked around the nearly dark room.

"The backup generator should kick on--" she announced and hesitated, "--now."

A few lights suddenly popped on along with the emergency exit signs. Hayes and young Riley were heard approaching from the Egyptian exhibit.

"I'll check the fuses," Hayes was heard saying.

Scarred Riley suddenly shoved Kane into a nearby, darkened alcove, startling him. She slammed him into the wall and pinned him against it with her body to avoid being seen by her younger self. Hayes and young Riley entered the exhibit.

"Forget to pay the electric bill?" young Riley teased.

"No." He then appeared to consider. "At least I think I did," Hayes remarked then snorted a laugh. "Why don't you wait in the lobby while I check the fuses in the basement?"

"Are you sure you don't need me to hold your hand?" she teased.

Hayes smiled slyly. "I may just take you up on that."

Riley and Hayes continued through the exhibit, passing Kane and Scarred Riley in the alcove, then entered the lobby. Scarred Riley looked at Kane while keeping him pressed against the wall with her body.

"I'm going to keep an eye on Hayes. You keep an eye on me," she hesitated, "the other me."

"Sure, but if you're going to hump him down there, do it quick, okay?" Kane remarked with his brows cleverly raised.

Scarred Riley glared at Kane through the dim lighting and sneered. "Seriously? You want to piss me off when I'm this close to your nuts?"

He was oddly silent a moment then gently cleared his throat and smirked. "Oh? And here I thought your hand was there on a purely social visit."

Scarred Riley glanced down at her hand clinging to his crotch, grinned lustfully, and met his gaze. "Bad habit."

Kane attempted to contain his boyish grin. "I actually wasn't complaining."

"I can tell," she teased and gently brushed her lips past his.

Scarred Riley firmly ran her hand along his crotch. Kane shut his eyes and groaned to her touch. This was definitely the sort of thing that never happened to him, and he intended to seize the opportunity. He grabbed her by the back of her neck and kissed her with passion and aggression, hoping she shared younger Riley's sexual desires. Without fail, she returned the wildly exotic kiss while groping him. They were the same woman! For a brief moment, all he could think about was having his way with her right there in the alcove; and how she was going to make *his* head spin. She suddenly broke off the kiss, took a quick step back, and stared at him with a look resembling concern. He stared back at her with surprise while attempting to control his heavy breathing.

"Are you okay?"

Her look immediately turned hostile. "I don't have time to waste humoring you," she scoffed. "I have to keep an eye on Hayes. He's the one who matters."

She turned away from him and disappeared into the dark corners of the exhibit. Kane sank against the wall, groaned lowly, and stared at the dark ceiling.

"What the hell is wrong with me?"

Chapter Thirty-four

*R*iley casually sat on the front desk in the quiet, dimly lit lobby. She wasn't bothered by the darkness or being alone in the museum after hours without lights. The museum was her home. She played with her cell phone, which gave off its own glow. Kane approached her and the desk from the next exhibit over. Riley saw him in the dim lighting, appeared surprised, and then relaxed when she realized who it was.

"Damn it, you scared me," she gasped softly. "I didn't think anyone else was here at this hour."

"I was in the west wing. Had one hell of a time finding my way back," he informed her. "Where's Hayes?"

"He went to check the fuses in the basement."

"Where's the security guard?" Kane asked with concern and uncertainly looked around.

"Andy? He's probably going for the fuses as well," she replied with little emotion.

There was an awkward silence. Kane stared at her. She gave him a second of eye contact then looked away and resumed loathing him. As he stared at her, he could no longer tell her apart from Scarred Riley. He wanted her so badly, but he knew it wasn't possible. This was the woman he loved, and he couldn't bear thinking she hated him. He couldn't leave it that way. He had to fix it. Kane groaned softly and leaned on the desk near her while holding his head.

"I screwed up, Riley." He looked at her even though she refused to look at him. "I, uh, I was in an 'on again off again' relationship with someone in the city. I, uh, just found out she might be pregnant. I need to do the right thing."

She now looked at him. "I see--"

"I never meant to hurt you, Riley. If I'd known that Connie--" He hesitated and reflected on an actual incident from his past, which really wasn't lying. "I never would have gotten involved with you if I knew we couldn't be together," he said softly and attempted to hold back the pain he felt. "I'd give anything to change it. I know you hate me, and you have every right to. I just hope you'll be able to forgive me one day."

Riley stared at him a moment in silence, slid off the desk, and put her arms around him. Kane shut his eyes and held her against him. She felt so good in his arms. He'd never felt this way, and he hated to admit it. He thought he loved Selena, but he suddenly realized he never knew what love was. He pulled away and met her gaze with tears in his eyes. He loved this woman so much, he knew there was only one thing he could do.

"Give Hayes a chance." He realized now that love was selfless, and he needed to do what was in Riley's best interest. "Hayes loves you. You were meant to be together."

"I'll keep that in mind."

Riley wiped the tears from his cheek and warmly kissed him on the lips. Kane hesitated then returned the warm kiss. It felt so good; he didn't want it to ever end. The kiss turned more passionate and aggressive, and it was Riley who initiated! For a moment, his head was swimming with thoughts of just moments ago in the mummy exhibit. As her hand firmly ran along his abdomen toward his pants, Kane broke off the kiss and pulled away.

"I can't do this," he suddenly announced then looked into her eyes with all seriousness, surprising her. "You deserve to know the entire truth, Riley. Five years from now--"

There was a distinctive thump from the dinosaur exhibit. Both suddenly looked across the dimly lit lobby and appeared concerned by the sound. There shouldn't have been anyone in that area.

"Did you hear that?" Riley asked.

"Yeah, it came from the exhibit next door. I'll have a look around," he said with concern. "I think you should lock yourself in Hayes' office."

She was obviously offended by the suggestion. "Maybe you're afraid of the dark, but I'm not."

Riley grabbed a baton style flashlight and headed across the lobby with a determined gait. Kane hurried after her and stopped her. His look was serious.

"That cave-in wasn't an accident," he suddenly blurted out while scanning her eyes.

Her look was stunned. "What?"

"Frank didn't rig the mine to explode," he quickly announced. "I think someone wanted you and Hayes out of the way."

"You can't be serious," Riley suddenly announced with a look of disbelief. "Who'd want to kill--?" Her look suddenly hardened. "Selena!"

"Selena's not capable of something like that," Kane remarked then considered the comment and frowned. "She's too much of a party girl."

"Think what you want, but I'm going to see who's lurking around next door," Riley announced firmly. "And then I'm going to deal with *her*."

Riley headed for the dinosaur exhibit with her imposing flashlight and a determined gait. Kane hurried after her.

†

*T*here were very few emergency lights in the nearly dark basement filled with stored exhibits that resembled clutter. Hayes walked along the cluttered storage area with his baton style flashlight. It wasn't the first time the lights had gone out, but it didn't happen often after hours. There was movement in the darkness. Hayes shined his light around and appeared concerned. He seemed a little more jumpy than usual.

"Riley? Is that you?" he asked while nervously clutching the flashlight. "No pouncing, okay?"

There was no response. Hayes uncertainly continued along the corridor with more caution. He shined the flashlight along the floor. There was a large streak of blood only a few feet from him. Hayes appeared alarmed and stopped.

"Riley? If you're down here, talk to me," he said nervously then looked around with the flashlight. "Andy?"

There was still no response. Hayes uncertainly followed the streak of blood trailing along the floor. It turned the corner. The security guard lie on the floor with blood surrounding his throat and shirt. Hayes gasped and removed his cell phone with trembling hands then immediately realized there was no signal.

"Basement--" Hayes gasped and uncertainly looked around for signs of the killer.

He turned and nearly collided with Scarred Riley. He cried out then held his chest. Once he caught his breath, he blurted out, "Andy is dead."

"I know; I saw him," Scarred Riley quickly replied in a hushed tone. "I'm going to follow you to your office. I want you to lock yourself in and call the police."

The alarm was evident on his face, and her seriousness wasn't helping. "What about Riley?"

"Kane is with her."

He studied her with a timid, fearful look. "What about you?" Hayes then asked.

She sneered in response. "I'm getting that bastard Tucker once and for all."

"Riley, no," he gasped softly and clung to her arm. "If anything happens to you--"

"It doesn't matter what happens to me," she remarked sternly with little emotion.

He stared at her with an odd look as his mouth hung open. "It matters to me."

Scarred Riley's harsh expression softened. She smiled lovingly and kissed him. "As long as my other self is alive, you won't lose me."

His look conveyed a different story, but he appeared defeated. "Be careful anyway," he said softly.

She smiled warmly, quickly kissed him on the lips, and hurried into the darkness.

Chapter Thirty-five

*R*iley walked past the displays with her flashlight while Kane walked behind her and cautiously looked around. He didn't like their situation. It seemed too convenient to be a coincidence. His pounding heart wasn't helping matters either. Part of him considered grabbing Riley and dragging her to safety against her will, but the rational part of him knew she could snap him in two if she felt threatened. Was it wrong that he was suddenly turned on? He quickly brushed those feelings aside.

"We should call the police," Kane announced softly.

"You're being paranoid."

A gunshot echoed through the room. Kane felt the sting of the bullet in his arm as he was thrown to the floor. Riley cried out and leaped to his fallen side. He clutched his bleeding arm in agony as she hovered over him.

"Still think I'm paranoid?"

Kane grabbed the flashlight from her hand and turned it off. There was another gunshot. He pulled Riley across the floor and behind an exhibit.

"I'm so sorry, Kane. I didn't know," she whispered with concern. "Are you okay?"

"If you don't mind, I'll wait to answer that," he gasped while cringing in pain.

Riley removed her cell phone and pressed a button. The face lit up the entire area around them. Kane gasped and concealed the light from the phone. A shot was fired and the bullet struck the exhibit in front of them.

"He can't see us without a light source."

"I'm sorry," she gasped. "I wasn't thinking."

The shooter moved within the darkness not far from them. Another figure suddenly appeared and tackled the shooter to the ground. An exhibit fell to the floor with a tremendous clatter. Kane knew their attacker was being kept busy by Scarred Riley, so he could send Riley to safety.

"Go to Hayes' office. Lock yourself in and call the police!" Kane cried out softly.

Riley nodded and ran across the exhibit. Kane grabbed the flashlight and turned it on then off to flush out the shooter. A gunshot was fired and nearly struck him. Scarred Riley's outline was seen as she kicked the gun from the man's hand. The gun flew across the floor. Young Riley stopped near the lobby archway to the sound of gunfire and looked back.

"Kane!" Riley yelled.

"Go!"

Riley ran into the lobby with her cell phone to her ear. She stopped to see Casper knocking on the glass doors in front. He smiled and waved at her. Riley was relieved and hurried for the doors. Casper suddenly appeared horrified and slammed his hands against the glass.

"Behind you!" Casper shouted.

Riley looked behind her. A figure in black lunged for her with a knife. Riley screamed, dropped her cell phone, and spun into a backwards roundhouse kick. The knife slashed her leg as her attacker was thrown backwards from her aggressive strike. Riley cried out while clutching her bleeding leg. The attacker came at her again. Casper was no longer seen at the door. Riley dove out of the path of the slashing knife. Hayes ran for them and tackled the figure in black to the floor. Both slid several feet and then rolled. Hayes and the attacker saw the discarded knife and lunged for it. The attacker grabbed it first and slashed Hayes across the arm. Hayes cried out and jumped back. The attacker lunged for his throat with the knife. The sound of a car's engine was heard followed by blinding headlights. All three looked to the glass windows as the black Mustang crashed through the glass doors and into the lobby. The

Mustang crashed into the front desk, exploding it, and spun to a screeching, spinning stop. Casper jumped out of his car. The figure in black ran out the broken entrance. Riley attempted to run after the attacker despite her limp. Hayes caught her around the waist and stopped her.

✝

Kane clutched the flashlight while on his hands and knees and felt around the floor for the gun in near darkness. Scarred Riley suddenly and silently appeared on the floor alongside him. Kane jumped with surprise, felt relieved to see it was just her, and then looked around.

"Where did he go?" Kane whispered.

"I don't know," Scarred Riley said softly.

"What was that crash?"

"Didn't you do that?" she asked with surprise.

"No, I thought it was you," he remarked then brushed it aside and looked around the dimly lit floor. "The gun's around here somewhere."

"Use the flashlight," she instructed. "Find the gun and protect Hayes and Riley."

"I can't just leave you--"

He could feel her eyes piercing through him despite the darkness. "Or you could stay and I can kick you in the nuts," she growled. "Choice is yours."

Kane groaned, reluctantly turned on the flashlight, and scanned the floor for the gun. Scarred Riley disappeared into the shadows. A figure in black suddenly leaped for Kane with a knife. Kane leaped out of his path and to his feet. The flashlight was still lit and lying on the floor. Kane looked around the shadows with concern then went for the flashlight. The attacker lunged with the knife for Kane's back. As Kane turned, Scarred Riley kicked Kane out of the attacker's path, placing herself between them. The attacker stabbed her in the side with the knife. She cried out in agony, but it didn't stop her from striking him with a powerful punch. He flew into the shadows. Scarred Riley clutched her bleeding side and stumbled backwards. Kane hurried for her.

"Find the gun!" Scarred Riley shouted despite her pain and the blood seeping through her fingers.

Kane leaped for the flashlight. The attacker again came at Scarred Riley. She kicked him in the face and then fell against an

175

exhibit without releasing her bleeding side. The attacker stumbled backwards, saw her in her weakened state, and lunged for her with the knife. Scarred Riley appeared unable to defend herself this time. The gun fired twice. The attacker took two shots to his body and fell to the floor. Kane held the gun and watched him fall. Scarred Riley half slid down the exhibit. Kane caught her and held her up and against him.

There were voices from the lobby. "Kane, are you okay?" young Riley was heard calling. "Someone's shooting at him in the dinosaur exhibit!"

Scarred Riley clung to Kane and her bleeding side while staring into his eyes. She was in genuine agony.

"She can't see me--" Scarred Riley gasped weakly.

Kane helped her into the dark alcove as young Riley, Hayes, and Casper ran across the exhibit and toward the fallen, masked attacker. Kane clung to Scarred Riley while holding her up against the wall with his body and kept pressure on her bleeding side. He searched her eyes in desperation to help her.

"We'll get you to the hospital," he said softly. "Let me call for an ambulance."

"It's too late for that," she said softly then smiled. "It's okay, really."

Hayes removed the killer's mask to reveal Collin. Collin gasped and spit up blood from the two, lethal gunshot wounds to his abdomen.

"Collin? Oh, my God," young Riley gasped.

"I don't believe it," Hayes said with surprise. "That doesn't make sense."

Young Riley looked around the darkened exhibit with concern. "Where's Kane? We have to find him!"

Casper grabbed the discarded flashlight and scanned the exhibit for his friend. "Kane?" he called while shining the light through the darkness.

Kane knew he couldn't answer him. They couldn't see Scarred Riley. She looked into Kane's eyes while panting, attempting to catch her breath.

"Collin?" Scarred Riley gasped softly with disbelief while searching Kane's eyes. "That's impossible. It was Tucker. It had to be Tucker."

"Try not to talk," Kane whispered softly to her.

Casper shined the light to the darkened alcove where Kane held Scarred Riley as she clung to him. As the flashlight stopped on them, Hayes looked as well. He stared at the alcove with a look of horror and uncertainly stood. Young Riley appeared oblivious and knelt alongside Collin as he slowly bled to death.

"Why did you do it, Collin?" Riley asked the dying man on the floor before her.

Collin stared into her eyes as blood seeped from his mouth. He looked as if he wanted to confess. Something in the way he stared at her was alarming.

"Never meant to hurt you," he gasped softly. "Just wanted Hayes gone."

"So you'd get his job?" she asked.

"Didn't know," he whispered faintly. "Wouldn't have hurt you."

Both Hayes and Casper stared at Kane holding the nearly lifeless Scarred Riley. Kane only looked at them briefly then returned his attention to the dying woman in his arms. Scarred Riley looked into Kane's eyes and touched his face.

"I remember the day we first met," Scarred Riley said softly while smiling.

"I forgive you, Riley," Kane said softly and was now down to tears.

Scarred Riley smiled lustfully while appearing peaceful and content. "There were broken pieces everywhere--"

Kane stared at Scarred Riley with a strange look. She appeared to be drifting out but maintained her smile.

"We spent the entire weekend in bed. You told me you loved me," she said softly.

Kane continued to stare at her with confusion and tears streaking his face. He smiled warmly while clinging to her and attempted to control his emotions.

"And I meant it," he whispered softly.

Scarred Riley kissed him warmly on the lips. Kane returned the kiss while holding back his sobs. It didn't seem possible, but he loved this woman and couldn't bear to lose her. She became lifeless in his arms. Kane pulled back and stared at her. Just like that, she was dead. He held her lifeless body against him and uncertainly looked across the room to Casper and Hayes, who were staring at him as he clung to her body. He had no business messing with the timeline, and now it didn't seem as if it was worth it. Young Riley remained kneeling over Collin, oblivious to the horror on Hayes and Casper's faces as they stared across the exhibit. Collin wheezed and never exhaled. His eyes remained opened and fixated on her. Riley stared at the motionless man on the floor before her.

"He's dead--" Riley softly informed them.

Kane held Scarred Riley in his arms, as tears streaked his face, and stared at Hayes and Casper across the darkened exhibit. Both men stared back at him in silence. There was a brilliant flash of light. Kane's entire life flashed before him in a thousand images and inaudible voices.

Chapter Thirty-six

*P*resent day. Light entered through the partially opened blinds in the massive bedroom decorated tastefully in antique furnishings. Kane clung to a woman beneath the covers while they slept. He woke, nuzzled the woman in his arms with a contented smile, and kissed the back of her neck. She moaned softly and turned to face him. Riley ran her hands along his chest and moved against him.

"Happy Anniversary," Riley said with a weary grin.

Kane kissed her warmly but passionately then pulled away while staring into her eyes.

"Are you sure you don't want to go somewhere exotic for our fourth anniversary? You know, as sort of a last hurrah," he teased warmly.

Riley suddenly flipped Kane onto his back, landed on top of him, and straddled his hips while hovering over him with a lustful smile as she pinned him to the bed.

"I'm still recovering from your last hurrah."

Kane smiled, looked at the small protrusion on her lower abdomen, and affectionately caressed it. He said to her belly, "Don't you listen to Mommy. That hurrah was all her." He grabbed Riley, threw her to the bed, and pinned her beneath him. "Now it's my turn."

Kane kissed Riley passionately and aggressively. She immediately returned the kiss. Making love to Riley was never an effort. Kane was convinced she possibly enjoyed their sexual antics more than he did. She'd ravish him anytime the mood struck her, make his head spin, and then go about her day. His life was perfect; and Riley was the reason for that.

✝

𝓕ive years ago. It was two days after Collin's death and the chaos at the museum. Casper read the headlines about the museum attack and shook his head. He glanced across the store and watched Kane in the back unpacking an antique china tea set. Casper frowned and lowered the paper. Kane was completely oblivious to it all. In a way, Casper almost missed that 'other' guy. Explaining how Casper's Mustang ended up in the museum lobby was a little tricky. He came up with an acceptable lie, which Hayes was more than willing to go along with to keep their time displacement secret. It was over, and somehow Casper had to put everything he'd been through with Kane from the future aside and go about life as usual. Eventually, he expected to read an engagement notice for Hayes and Riley. Perhaps they'd even invite him to the wedding. Kane was oblivious that he would miss the woman he loved; yet never knew he'd even met. Casper knew it was for the best. In three years, he'd meet Selena, and it would be Casper's job to work out the bugs created by Kane's future self. Casper desperately needed to get back to work and put all this time travel behind him. He leaned on the front desk and jotted notes on a tablet. The bell above the door dinged. As the door opened, Casper looked up. His expression immediately dropped. Riley and Hayes entered the antique store. Riley limped from her leg injury and relied on Hayes to assist her. Casper quickly approached Hayes with surprise and possible concern then looked at Riley, who smiled sweetly at him.

"Hi, Casper. Is he here?" she asked.

"I, uh, I don't know--" he said while looking frantically between her and Hayes.

"It's okay, Casper," Hayes informed him while nodding reassuringly. "She knows everything."

"Yeah, but, he doesn't," Casper protested softy. "He had nothing to do with--"

Hayes pointed across the shop and guided Riley past Casper toward the back. She clung to his arm while limping alongside him. The injury from her attack in the museum just two days earlier was healing, but she was obviously in pain. They approached Kane as he turned with the antique china tea set. The tea set slipped from the tray and crashed to the floor, shattering into a million pieces. Kane saw Riley, stared at her, and then smiled with embarrassment.

"I'm so sorry. I didn't get you, did I?" Kane asked mostly to Riley.

Riley smiled warmly and shook her head. Kane stared at her longer than he should. He'd never seen this woman before, but she was absolutely stunning. A thousand thoughts raced through his mind. Not a single one was appropriate. She stared back with the most radiant smile. He almost felt as if she was undressing him with her eyes. He'd never experienced something like that before, but he actually liked it.

"Kane Maddox? I'm Hayes Dante, the museum curator," Hayes announced while smiling pleasantly and snapped him out of his hormone-induced trance.

Casper uncertainly moved closer with his mouth hanging open and watched the unfolding scene with concern. Kane shook Hayes' hand and attempted to keep from staring at the beautiful woman on his arm.

"It's a pleasure to meet you, Mr. Dante," Kane said and again allowed his eyes to travel over the beautiful woman. He looked away almost shameful of his thoughts.

"This is my assistant, Riley Jericho," Hayes cheerfully introduced her.

Kane's attention immediately shifted back to the beautiful woman on Hayes' arm. Riley extended her hand to Kane and smiled affectionately. Kane immediately accepted her hand, again stared longer than he probably should, and appeared reluctant to release her hand.

"It's a pleasure, Ms. Jericho," he said almost timidly.

"Your associate--" Hayes said and indicated Casper, who stared at them with a dumbfounded expression, "--told me about some amazing antique pieces that would be perfect for an exhibit we're working on."

"I did?" Casper asked.

"Riley will tell you all about it while Casper shows me around the store," Hayes announced while grabbing Casper's arm and quickly pulled him away.

"But, I, what--?"

Kane appeared embarrassed and looked at the broken china on the floor. He chuckled softly and ran his fingers through his hair while smiling at Riley. "Well, I've certainly made better first impressions."

Riley looked into his eyes while smiling. "I think you're doing just fine--"

Kane fidgeted then relaxed and returned the smile. He never believed in love at first sight, but he was suddenly convinced it could happened. This was the woman he knew he'd someday marry. Although it didn't seem possible, by the way she was looking at him, he was convinced she knew it too.

Chapter Thirty-seven

*P*resent day. Casper stood behind the desk in the antique store with his cell phone to his ear. By the look on his face, he appeared excited about the phone call he'd received.

"That's awesome. I'm looking forward to it. I'll see you then," Casper said.

Casper disconnected the call and set his cell phone down as Kane approached the desk from the back room. He appeared unusually distracted while holding up two wallpaper swatches.

"Who was that?"

"Oh, just your Nana," Casper replied. "She invited me and Bessie for dinner this weekend."

Kane looked at Casper, smiled with something resembling humor, and shook his head. "I think I'm being replaced as her grandson," he teased.

"Don't be silly," Casper announced cheerfully. "She just loves feeding me."

"Well, I think it's lucky for us you took that CPR course and just happened to stop by her house after her birthday party," Kane remarked and marveled while shaking his head. "You probably saved her life that night."

"Yeah, maybe. Right place; right time," he replied with a disinterested shrug and secretly smirked. "I can't believe you used that money she gave you to buy one third interest in this place. You could have paid off your house with that money."

Kane shrugged. "There's nothing wrong with having a mortgage these days. Besides, Hayes was enthusiastic to loan us the money at a low interest rate."

Casper watched Kane, who studied the swatches. He seemed overly serious as he compared the two swatches. "What are you doing now?"

Kane glanced at both swatches in his hands. "Riley wants me to pick out the wallpaper for the nursery, but I can't decide between bunnies and kittens," he announced with a defeated sigh.

Casper eyed the swatches then stared at Kane with all seriousness. "Dude, they're both bunnies."

Kane was puzzled by the comment and looked at both with surprise. "Are you sure?"

"Yes, I'm sure."

Kane set the swatches down and looked at the objects scattered along the desk. The smashed copper trinket box was among them. Kane uncertainly picked it up and looked over it with surprise to its condition.

"What happened to this?"

"Oh--" Casper smiled timidly. "I kind of sort of ran over it with the truck, you know, kind of *accidentally*. Whatever--it was junk anyway."

Kane tossed it down on the desk with little interest and returned to his swatches. "We certainly don't need more trinket boxes anyway."

"My thoughts exactly," Casper replied with a sly grin. "You, uh, tell Riley about the trip to Hawaii yet?"

"I tried to this morning," he announced then grinned and raised his brows lustfully, "but she *distracted* me."

"Well, she is rather distracting," Casper announced with a cheap grin.

"I already cleared her time off at the museum with Hayes. His girlfriend thinks Riley's going through the whole nesting faze a little early," Kane announced. "I think she's just stressed with everything at work."

"Is Selena being a bitch to her again?"

"Selena specializes in bitchiness. She's always been jealous of Riley," Kane remarked then shook his head. "You know, I never liked that girl."

"Yeah, me either. She keeps insisting that we'd met at some fundraiser at the museum and spent three days at Bessie's bed and breakfast. I think I'd remember something like that," Casper informed him.

Kane gave him a bewildered look. "She used to tell me that all the time too."

Casper appeared humored and chuckled softly. "No kidding? What a nut job."

"I'll tell you what her problem is," Kane remarked boldly. "It's that on again off again relationship with that security guard, Tucker. He's brings out the worst in her."

"Hayes should fire his ass," Casper remarked.

"His hands are tied," Kane announced. "He has no grounds for dismissal."

✝

*J*illian hung out with Chrissie at the front desk in the museum lobby. They appeared to be softly gossiping and immediately silenced when Selena approached. Selena gave each woman a stern, irritated look.

"Did I interrupt something?" Selena suddenly asked.

"No, not at all," Chrissie reported and appeared to be hiding something from her friend.

Selena stared at both women and didn't seem convinced. "You guys are supposed to be my friends. What's going on? If you heard some good gossip, I want to know."

"Well," Jillian began and immediately silenced.

"We just learned from Hayes that Riley is only taking a few weeks maternity leave after the baby is born," Chrissie announced. "Apparently, Hayes worked something out to provide daycare here in the museum."

Selena took a deep breath and shook her head. "I'm not surprised," she remarked with a soft groan. "He can't live three days without her. I thought his girlfriend would have cured him of that little crush."

"His girlfriend adores Riley," Jillian announced.

"I can't believe Hayes has been dating Dr. Melbourne's sister nearly a year now," Chrissie remarked. "I wonder when Melbourne's coming for another visit." She appeared dreamy. "He smiled at me the last time he stopped by."

Selena rolled her eyes and groaned. "Personally, I'd rather not run into him again."

"Oh, that's right," Chrissie announced with a soft gasp. "I'm so sorry, Selena. I forgot about that incident with you and Dr. Melbourne five years ago."

"What incident?" Jillian asked with surprise. "Did I miss something?"

"You remember when Dr. Melbourne attended his first fundraiser here," Chrissie reminded Jillian. "Selena and Melbourne hooked up afterwards and he never called her."

"Oh, that," Jillian said and waved it off.

"Please, let's stop reliving the past!" Selena looked at her watch and then the clock. "Well, I'm out of here early tonight. Tucker and I have plans."

As if on cue, Tucker quickly approached the desk while grinning. "Save the gossip for another time," he announced. "We have plans tonight."

She flashed a lustful smile at both women while clinging to Tucker. "The spa won't hold our reservations forever," Selena teased then joined Tucker.

Both women watched them leave the museum.

Chrissie shook her head with disgust. "She could do so much better."

"I can't believe they're actually still together," Jillian announced with a groan then eyed Chrissie. "What's the story about her romp with Melbourne? She's slept with plenty of men who've never called her back."

Chrissie leaned in closer and grinned. "She tried to hook him with a false pregnancy, but, apparently, Dr. Melbourne got snipped years ago."

"Oh, my God!" Jillian gasped. "I didn't hear that."

"Of course you didn't," Chrissie replied. "She was totally embarrassed by it. Tucker still believes she didn't sleep with Melbourne until after he dumped her at that bed and breakfast. He's so dense."

"What's going on in that girl's head lately?" Jillian suddenly asked.

"Why? Did you hear something?"

Jillian grinned, lustfully raised her brows, and leaned on the desk. "I heard she recently made several pretty serious sexual advances at Hayes."

"You mean more than usual?" Chrissie asked and giggled at her friend's expense. "She's been throwing herself at him for years."

"He should fire her," Jillian said. "I'd be an excellent candidate for Selena's position."

"The line forms behind me," Chrissie snorted while glaring at her friend.

Jillian gave her a look of surprise then appeared irritated. "Says who?"

✝

*I*t was after closing time, and the museum lobby was dimly lit. Just about everyone had gone home for the night, and the place seemed eerily quiet. Howard, the security guard, opened the door and allowed Kane to enter.

"Evening, Kane," Howard greeted him cheerfully.

"Hey, Howard."

Kane looked around the creepy, quiet lobby and shook his head. The museum after hours always gave Kane the creeps. He remembered reading about the murder of that security guard and the attack on Riley and Hayes. That was just two days before he met and fell in love with Riley. He had to give credit to Howard. He didn't know how he could work there alone at night after what had happened. The place was creepy enough without the brutal attack.

"Aren't you worried one of the dinosaurs will come back to life and eat you?" Kane asked the security guard while grimacing.

"Be serious, Kane," Howard announced then grinned. "I'd have a heart attack long before one of those walking skeletons could ever eat me."

Kane chuckled. "Is Riley ready?"

"I don't know, but she's the last one here. You need to take that girl home," Howard informed him with a serious look. "She works too late for someone in her condition."

Kane appeared to hesitate and eyed Howard. Something suddenly seemed off. He uncertainly shook his head and managed a smile. "Yeah, I hear you."

"Is something wrong?" Howard asked.

"It's strange," Kane said while tilting his head. "I'm having this weird feeling of Deja vu."

"I know what you mean," Howard replied then grinned. "Of course, all my days are exactly the same."

Kane remained tense and attempted to shake the feeling. "Where is she?"

"In the Egyptian exhibit, I believe."

Kane stared at Howard and suddenly appeared alarmed. He wasn't sure what was wrong, but he had a terrible feeling. Kane ran across the lobby and through the dinosaur exhibit. He didn't slow through the dinosaurs and headed straight for the Egyptian exhibit. As Kane ran into the room, the sound of a gunshot rang out and echoed across the room. Kane gasped, ran toward the back, and skidded to a stop. Selena lie on the floor with blood soaking her shirt. A gun lie near her outstretched hand. Hayes stood over Selena's body with his own gun and stared blankly at her. Kane looked across the room at Riley. She clung to her baby bump and stared at Selena's lifeless body with the horror evident on her face. Kane ran to Riley. A man dressed in black wearing a mask suddenly darted past them and for the exhibit entrance.

"Kane," Riley cried out.

Without hesitation, Kane spun into a high, roundhouse kick and struck the man in the chest, sending him roughly to the floor. He writhed in agony. For once, Kane was glad he'd spent all those weekends with Riley's crazy uncle. Hayes, Riley, and Kane approached the groaning man. Kane grabbed Riley and prevented her from getting too close to the man on the floor. Hayes knelt alongside the man and removed his mask to reveal Tucker. Neither Hayes nor Riley seemed too surprised. Kane was stunned while clinging to Riley.

"I don't understand. What happened?" Kane asked and felt as if he was the only one who didn't know what was going on.

Riley uncertainly shook her head and again looked at the dead woman several feet away. "I thought she'd gone home, but she showed up with a gun. She wanted to kill me," Riley announced then looked at Hayes. "It was her, wasn't it? Five years ago when Collin tried to kill you, she was the one in the lobby who slashed me. They were in on it together. She wanted me out-of-the-way, so she could have my position. That's what Collin meant. He didn't know Selena intended to kill me all along."

"I suspect she was behind everything," Hayes remarked. "I think you were always the intended target. Collin and Tucker were just her unwitting pawns. They did her bidding without ever seeing her hidden agenda. She wanted your position and my money." Hayes shook his head and stared at Tucker, who remained on the floor staring up at him. "Unfortunately for them, some of us are better equipped to predict the future than others."

Hayes' cell phone rang. The caller ID read 'Casper'. Hayes looked at Kane, who held Riley, and flashed a tiny smile. "And there's my crystal ball now."

Hayes handed Kane his gun then answered the phone as he walked away. Kane clung to Riley while keeping the gun trained on Tucker as Howard ran into the exhibit while removing his own gun. He was slow to the party as usual.

Riley finally looked at Kane as he held her and forced a tiny, nervous smile. "I think I'd like to take you up on that romantic getaway now."

Fade Out

Other books by Holly Copella!
Reviews left on Amazon are appreciated!

"The Battle for Andrea Maria"

A cruise ship attack turns six survivors into overnight celebrities after they take credit for the heroic act of a stowaway who died saving them.

The cruise is just what Jess needed--a bit of harmless fun far from her daily grind. But what begins as a relaxing vacation turns into a desperate fight for her life when terrorists take over the ship and start piling up bodies. Teaming up with a mysterious stowaway, Jess attempts to send out a distress call but knows they cannot wait for help to come. If she or the few remaining passengers have any hope for survival, Jess must act now. The papers dub it "The Battle for *Andrea Maria*," but to Jess it is the moment she fought side-by-side with her enigmatic Romeo, saving the ship--and losing him. She thinks the story ends there, but really, the nightmare is just beginning...

"Insanely Deadly"

When the dead return to life, it's up to an admiral's daughter and a mildly insane, former war hero to save their small town.

Jetta Cross, a Navy Admiral's daughter, is tasked with keeping her father's comrade, a former war hero turned town crazy, grounded in the real world. Capt. John Hunter is still fighting the war in his head, where imaginary dead people are part of his world. When a viral outbreak brings about a zombie uprising, Hunter is left to his own devices. He must resume his role as a one-man commando unit in order to destroy the ravenous undead. With Hunter still fighting his own inner demons as well as the undead, the townspeople fear their zombie neighbors may not be the only threat. Stranded at the island's luxurious resort with a handful of workers, Jetta is forced to live up to her father's reputation and take charge of the deteriorating situation at the hotel. She must wage her own war against the infected before the government declares her hometown a total loss.

"Deadly Institution"

A town recluse suspected of killing his wife teams up with a young woman in order to stop a killer.

After being accused of murdering his wife, Konrad Asher turns his back on the town that once adored him. Ten years later, he still holds his grudge and the title of the most feared man in town. With the reopening of the burned mental institution, where his wife had died, former employees are now murdered one-by-one, throwing suspicion back on Asher. A young local reporter, Jacey, is forced to reveal her long-time friendship with the infamous recluse in order to clear his name not only in the recent murders but to exonerate him in the death of his wife as well. Will Jacey's relationship with Asher invite the killer closer to her? Or is the killer already in her life?

"Town Darling"

After surviving a brutal attack that claims the lives of those she loves, a young woman seeks revenge on a corrupt town.

Going back home is never easy, but for Casey, it means returning to her corrupt hometown where she barely survived a brutal attack. Accompanied by two *family friends*, she seeks justice for the night that destroyed her life. Her physical scars are nothing compared to her emotional ones, forcing the local sheriff to believe that the town darling is back for revenge. As the conspiracy for her revenge appears to be leading up to the coveted town fair, the sheriff is determined to stop her from fulfilling her vengeful scheme...but guilt over his role on that fateful night continues to haunt him. His desperate need for Casey's forgiveness could be his undoing.

"Screenplays: The Island Collection"
"Jungle Princess", "A.L.F. Resort", "Brighton Island"

Discover how romance and fun in the sun can be downright *chilling*!

"Jungle Princess" is a romantic/thriller that leaves a teenage girl stranded on an island with two male shipmates and a creature of "unknown" origin. She soon discovers the island is home to an abandoned prison with several prisoners roaming free. What really killed over one hundred prisoners? And is it still out there--?

"A.L.F. Resort" is a romantic/thriller set on an island resort with Artificial Life Forms as the main draw. At this resort, all your fantasies come true...until a malfunction removes safety inhibitors on the A.L.F.'s. Zombies, biker gangs, and mobsters run amuck, turning fantasies into nightmares. A young reporter gets more of a story than she anticipates, but will she survive long enough to write the story?

"Brighton Island" is a romantic/thriller set on a private island. When the owner's niece brings her psychic friend to the mansion, his presence awakens the spirits' tortured souls. As the psychic attempts to solve the old murders, the niece is confronted with the possibility that she's next to join the mansion ghosts. Stranded on the island with a crazed killer, he uncle wages his own war to save them. Will his "shock and awe" tactics actually save them or get them killed?

ABOUT THE AUTHOR

Holly Copella has been writing since the age of twelve when her frustration at a book's poor plot drove her to author her own story. Over the last decade, she's written a number of screenplays, some of which she's now adapting into novels. Her fascination with zombies and other darker material lends an edge to her writing, which tends to lean toward horror. As a fan of Agatha Christie, she appreciates the craft of a good plot and the importance of creating significant characters.

Hailing from Pennsylvania, Copella lives in the Endless Mountains on a farm with her rescue horses and other animals. In addition to writing and reading fiction, she enjoys riding horses and traveling to Las Vegas and Disney World.

www.ingramcontent.com/pod-product-compliance
Lightning Source LLC
Chambersburg PA
CBHW061121180626
46811CB00012BB/737